# IN THE LIMELIGHT

Beth Telford, the practical member of a family entertaining troupe, Telford Tourers, was content to take a backstage role until handsome Angus Lancaster became a regular member of the audience and subsequently joined the players. His appearance coincides with a series of disasters for Telford Tourers, but these are nothing compared with the shock that awaits the family when Angus reveals his true identity with a tale far more dramatic than anything they ever presented on stage.

JOYCE JOHNSON

# IN THE LIMELIGHT

*Complete and Unabridged*

# LINFORD
*Leicester*

First published in Great Britain in 2002

First Linford Edition
published 2004

British Library CIP Data

Johnson, Joyce, *1931 –*
    In the limelight.—Large print ed.—
Linford romance library
    1. Love stories
    2. Large type books
    I. Title
    813.5′4 [F]

ISBN 1–84395–364–1

Published by
F. A. Thorpe (Publishing)
Anstey, Leicestershire

Set by Words & Graphics Ltd.
Anstey, Leicestershire
Printed and bound in Great Britain by
T. J. International Ltd., Padstow, Cornwall

This book is printed on acid-free paper

# 1

Beth Telford scrunched her handkerchief into a ball and rubbed the misted glass of the carriage windows. Nose pressed against the cold glass, she peered out at the outside world but couldn't see anything beyond the piled-up snowflakes driving against the window. She shivered, knotted her thick, woollen scarf more securely round her throat and pulled her hat well down over her ears. Nothing for it but to leave the shelter of the carriage and venture outside to see what was happening.

Outside was a blinding, whirling snow mass and her feet sank ankle deep into the stuff.

A few moments earlier the carriage had suddenly swerved and stopped, the horses refusing to budge a step farther.

'Dad,' she called out, 'where are you,

and where are we?'

'I'm sorry, girl, but we didn't expect this to blow up. Fine enough when we left Leeds.'

She raised her voice, still unable to see anything.

'Dad, Nat, Jim, where are you?'

She jumped as a hand grasped her shoulder.

'Nat, thank goodness. I thought you'd abandoned ship and me with it.'

'Not likely,' the tall young man replied as he took her arm. 'You should get back inside. It's bitter out here.'

'I'm fine, well wrapped up as you see. Where have Dad and Jim got to?'

'Round the other side by Nelly. The horses' hooves are clogged with snow. They could slip if they aren't cleared.'

'We'll never make Brancaster in time for the performance. The others will be worried about us.'

'They'll guess the snow slowed us down, and they'll be snug as bugs going by train. We picked the short straw.'

'Someone had to bring the carriage

and I think this is more fun, apart from the worry if we'll be in time for curtain up.'

'If we don't, we don't. We'll only miss a couple of items and the hand-bell ringing won't matter if there are two of us short. And your mother can keep an audience entertained on her own for hours. This sort of delay's bound to happen from time to time. One of the hazards of touring.'

Beth stamped her feet to keep warm and considered there were more hazards than just the weather facing the Telford Tourers. Dwindling audiences, rising costs and finally arguments were just a few. The family had been on the road, on and off, for nearly ten years now. Beth's mother, Constance, had started it all off as a joke, she'd said, after a very successful village pantomime. Beth had been twelve, Julia thirteen, little Clarice barely a toddler and the twins, Will and Henry, nine.

It had been wonderfully exciting to begin with, especially no school, although Aunt Eva who travelled with them made sure they all had regular lessons, and journeying throughout England had certainly taught them many valuable life lessons. Yet she had felt lately that Julia and the boys were wanting to develop their own lives and were pulling in different directions. How much longer they could put up with the wandering minstrel life, she couldn't guess.

A figure loomed out of the snow.

'You two give us a hand. We're nearly done, just a final check. If you hold one of the horse's heads each Jim and I can make sure we've cleaned the impacted snow. The road's clearer ahead.'

'Mr Telford, Beth should be in the carriage. She'll catch her death of cold out here,' Nat reproved.

'Don't fuss,' Beth said. 'I'm warm as toast.'

Bernard Telford patted his daughter's shoulder.

'We can always depend on you, Beth. Now, you take Nelly, and Nat, you take

Daisy here. We'll soon be on the move.'

Father and daughter moved arm in arm round to Nelly.

'This is no life for a girl like you,' Nat muttered under his breath. 'It's just not good enough,' he called after her but his words were blown away.

The party arrived at Stanwell Road Temperance Hall just thirty minutes after curtain up on the Telford Tourers' Christmas Special concert. Outside the hall, Jim Benson nodded his head as the clear tones of the first item rang through the frosty air.

'Grand bit of bell ringing,' he said as his passengers hurried out. 'You've trained them well, Bernard.'

He flicked the reins over the horses' ears.

'Be with you as soon as I've stabled these two. Horse and Hounds, wasn't it?'

'Yes, all arranged,' Beth replied as she and her father hurried to the side entrance of the hall, Nat following with their bags.

In a small ante-room which served for changing and storing props and instruments a tall, silver-haired woman was hanging coats on a rail.

'Aunt Eva,' Beth said as she kissed her, 'we've had such a journey.'

'I can well imagine. Atrocious weather, but you're here now and things are going fine. Your ma charmed them all into submission in the first few minutes.'

'As she always can.'

Beth struggled into a silk plaid dress.

'Brr, I'll need a jacket over this, it's so cold.'

'It's warmer in the hall. There, bell ringing's done. Hear the clapping? Constance's solo next. I've seen to the piano, right up to pitch, so get ready to go on.'

Applause continued as four more Telfords came into the room. Julia hugged Beth.

'Glad you made it. Mother's frantic. Had you all dead and buried in a snow drift.'

'Always one for high drama,' Eva

Telford said wryly. 'Go on, Beth.'

Will and Henry, the eighteen-year-old identical twins gave her a friendly push towards the stage.

'Good luck, Sis.'

'Oh, dear, I haven't had a run-through!'

The rest of her volatile family loved performing on stage, even Bernard, a farmer by birth, profession and inclination, lapped up the applause for his rural monologues, but Beth always suffered from stage-fright. Her main function was general organiser and stage manager but she was the best pianist in the family and Constance Telford's beautiful soprano voice deserved only the best.

'My fingers are frozen,' she procrastinated as Will and Henry literally pushed her on to the stage.

Her mother's warm, welcoming smile gave her confidence and as soon as she began to play, as usual, she enjoyed being the instrument for showing off her mother's voice. Constance's solo was well received and an encore was insisted on.

The whole performance went swimmingly as the audience caught the Christmas spirit, cheering, clapping and stamping their feet in appreciation. They joined in the carols to round off the evening and even Beth was pulled into the atmosphere, smiling and bowing like a real trouper as the final curtain swished across.

The festive and euphoric mood continued at Mrs Earnshaw's theatrical lodging house, lasting throughout the excellent steak-and-kidney pie and ale. The troupe members were Mrs Earnshaw's regulars and nothing was too good for them. Constance, as usual, was the focal point of the party.

'Wasn't it splendid tonight, Bernard?' she said, eyes sparkling. 'I was worried though when you weren't at the station. I imagined you . . .'

'All dead under a snowdrift. I know, my dear. Well, I'm not. We're here, you were magnificent and it was the best

8

house we've had in weeks.'

He laid his arm across her shoulder as she turned to him, their passion for each other sparking like struck flint-stones.

Twenty-two years earlier, Bernard had met the beautiful, dark-haired Constance in London on one of his regular trips to Smithfield livestock market. Instantly, farming business was forgotten and his urgent priority was to persuade Constance to exchange her comfortable, sophisticated city life for the harsher life of a farmer's wife in the remote Yorkshire Dales.

He never ceased to marvel she had accepted him in the first place and that the marriage, in spite of its ups and downs, had worked. There had been sacrifices, compromises, even bitter arguments on some issues, but their love had sustained and grown more passionate with the years.

The noise level in Mrs Earnshaw's dining-room grew louder as the family, plus Nat and Jim, tucked into the excellent meal. The landlady brought in more vegetables and another jug of ale.

'As it's near Christmas and you'll not be off tomorrow at the crack of dawn,' she justified the extra jug.

Constance smiled.

'You spoil us, and isn't it lovely that we'll be staying with you an extra night?'

'I hope the business will warrant it.'

Beth, ever the practical one, frowned. The Tourers usually played only one night at each venue, sometimes giving two performances afternoon and evening before travelling on to the next place.

'Beth, you're a wet blanket,' Julia admonished. 'I bet tonight's audience come again and bring their friends with them. You'll see.'

'Let's hope so. We've another week before we . . . '

She stopped. Why was Nat looking at her so intently? Did he also think she was a wet blanket? She gave him a friendly wink which he didn't return. It was Bernard who finished her sentence.

'Before we go back to the farm, you mean?'

The silence which followed was a marked contrast to the previous babble, as if the curtain had fallen prematurely on the first act of a comedy. Nat continued to stare at Beth and Beth looked at Constance who was watching Bernard. The moment held, the family suspended, then Constance gave a deep, telling sigh. She turned her large dark eyes on her husband.

'Bernard, nothing's been decided yet. We've hardly had time to talk it's been such a busy run up to Christmas. We've all worked so terribly hard.'

'We could all do with a rest, and I need to spend some time at Pikesfell, see how Alf's doing.'

'Splendidly,' Constance exclaimed. 'Didn't he write and tell you so only last week?'

'I need to see for myself. It's nearly two years since we've been back home for any length of time.'

Constance laid a hand on his arm.

'Dearest, shouldn't we find out what everyone else wants to do? The children may have their own plans. They're grown up now. They should have a say in the future. Jim and Nat will want to go back to the village to see their friends and family at Christmas, so Jim can report back on the condition of the farm.'

Now the full force of her expressive eyes swept reproachfully over the entire company.

'And what about me? Don't I deserve a little thoughtfulness?'

There was a pause. Bernard looked crestfallen. Julia jumped up and went to hug Constance in comfort.

'Of course you do. I don't mind what we do so long as you're happy. What would you like to do?'

There was a perfectly-timed, dramatic pause before Constance clasped her hands together, stretched them away in front of her and regarded her elegant fingers.

'I should very much like to go to London for Christmas.'

'London!' Bernard was horrified. 'What on earth for?'

'London!' Julia echoed. 'How wonderful. Dad, can we, please? We can always go to the farm later and I've never been to London.'

'You're not missing much, my girl. Noisy, busy place, with smelly motor cars, too many people.'

'But we'd like the chance to see for ourselves,' the twins chimed in unison. 'Go on, it'd be a lark. Better than playing Birmingham last Christmas.'

'Haven't we had enough larks during the year?' Bernard said. 'A slice of rural peace and quiet would do my soul good.'

'But, dear, it would be fun,' Constance said enthusiastically. 'I haven't been to London for five years. It was my home before I met you. Please, as a big favour.'

Constance's velvety voice wheedled seductively, and Beth watched with interest. Her mother always got her own way in the end but now she wasn't so sure. Constance was ten years younger than Bernard and lately he'd shown signs that the endless travelling and hectic pace of the Tourers' schedule was beginning to show.

He was slower, complained of backache and talked more longingly of his farm, managed in his absence by his younger brother, Alf. Beth watched with a stirring of apprehension. Something told her changes were on the horizon. London or the farm for Christmas? It was a big issue and both sides looked set to dig in. It was Aunt Eva who suggested the compromise.

'Would it be so terrible if we split up for Christmas? I'm happy to go to the farm with Bernard and the rest could go up to town, just for a holiday.'

'What? Separate at Christmas? We've never done that. Constance, you'd hate that, surely?'

Bernard appealed to his wife in dismay.

'Well, it would be awful but as you hate the idea of London and, Bernard, it's so cold at Pikesfell. I'd so love to see some shows. There's a new play at Drury Lane, and there's the shopping, the department stores.'

She leaned over and put her arm round Bernard's neck.

'Please, please, we'd all love it.'

'Not me,' young Clarrie spoke up. 'I want to see Holly and the rabbits and Porky. I don't want to go to London one bit.'

'Beth?' Constance appealed.

'I'm not sure. London would be fun but I was looking forward to the farm, riding Starlight, walking the fells. I miss the peace and feeling settled.'

'Boring,' Will sang out.

'Looks like a majority then,' Constance said quickly. 'We'll all go to London for Christmas.'

'No,' Bernard exclaimed. 'I'll not go, but those who want to can. As Eva said, you four are old enough to make up your own minds. Clarice, Eva and I,

15

maybe Beth, we'll go to Pikesfell. It's good to break the routine once in a while,' he added rather sadly.

'London, London,' Julia sang and danced around the table. 'Mother, you're a genius. Dad, you're an angel. What shows can we see? Where shall we stay? What'll I wear?'

'We can think about all that tomorrow. Best settle down and go to bed now. It's late and we've had a long day with a busy one ahead. Jim, Nat, you'd best be off. Mrs Earnshaw's sister's two doors down. She'll put you up as usual.'

Nat hung back and said, 'I'd like a word with Beth.'

'Can't it wait until morning, Nat?' Beth yawned. 'If it's those lights you're worried about . . . '

'No, nothing to do with the show. Personal,' Nat said and pointed to the twins who showed no signs of heeding the call to bed.

Will upended the ale jug into a couple of glasses.

'Go ahead, Nat, don't mind us.'

16

'I do mind though. I want to talk to Beth in private.'

Fortunately, Bernard called downstairs that the bathroom was free and the twins were to come up immediately. Nat sighed with relief as he shut the door firmly behind them.

'What's the problem?' Beth asked.

Now that he had her attention, Nat seemed reluctant to speak. He fiddled with his collar, coughed, and looked at the floor, anywhere but at Beth.

'Well?' she encouraged.

He took a breath, looked up, blinked, and then spoke.

'I can't keep quiet any longer. I know I'll die if I don't speak out.'

'What? Oh, dear, it sounds serious. Are you sick?'

'I am — lovesick for you, Beth. You must know how I feel about you, all the years we've known each other, even at school in the village. I want us to be married. I can't stand working so close to you and not be able to . . . to touch you . . . to kiss you.'

17

'Nat, stop!'

Beth stood up in agitation.

'I don't know what to say. I had no idea of any of this. I thought you and I were such good friends. I've always relied so much on you.'

'Why do you think I joined the Tourers?' Nat burst out. 'When Dad retired from the blacksmith's I could have taken over. I enjoy working with horses. After Ma died Dad had this mad notion to join your family so I seized my chance. I'd missed you so much while you were away.'

'Nat! I'm sorry. I can't think what to say, it's all so strange.'

'Beth?' her father called down.

'Nat, it's so late,' she began, but he took her hand and put it to his lips.

'If I've shocked you, I'm sorry. I was certain you must have had some inkling, but don't refuse me. I don't know what I'd do if you do. I'll do everything to make you happy, stay with the Tourers if that's what you want or go back to Pikesfell, buy some land nearby, farm.'

Beth disengaged her hand, her head a teeming torrent of confused thoughts. It truly was a shock to hear Nathan Benson speak in such a way. She'd never considered him in a romantic light. The very thought made her blush. She looked at him. He was good-looking, without a doubt, strong with a straight back and broad shoulders.

'Beth!' her father's voice called again, more peremptory.

'You'll have to go, Nat. I must do as Father wishes.'

'You're a grown woman, old enough to marry and be your own mistress. You're too possessed by your family, Beth.'

It had never felt like that but maybe he was right. She'd never thought of a life beyond the Telford Tourers, and as for a life with Nathan, well . . .

'I've always thought of us like brother and sister,' she said slowly.

He put his arms around her and pulled her to him.

'I want to be far more than that. I can make you love me if you don't already.'

He kissed her on the lips. She allowed a brief contact, not disliking the sensation. With it came the thought she'd never been kissed like that before by a man. She drew back.

'You must go. We'll talk tomorrow. I must think.'

'But I can hope, can't I?' he pleaded.

Beth felt the unfamiliar pull of physical attraction. It unnerved her. All she wanted was for Nat to go, to leave her alone to sort out these unfamiliar feelings.

'I suppose, but go now, at once, or Father will throw you out.'

He kissed her again lightly, his eyes burning.

'Dear Beth, you've made me the happiest man in England.'

'But I've not said . . . I need to think. You can't . . . '

'Beth, what are you doing down there? Hasn't Nat gone yet?' her father yelled and there were footsteps on the stairs as Nat closed the front door.

'Yes, Father, Nat's gone and I'm just coming up to bed.'

# 2

Beth slid into the bed she shared with Julia, who was already sound asleep. It was impossible for her to sleep after what Nat had said. What a surprise, and shock! Could she have unknowingly led him on?

Although astounded when he joined Telford Tourers she'd been delighted. He was an ally, an extra pair of reliable and willing hands, so of course she'd encouraged him to stay on. Obviously he'd mistaken her pleasure for love, not friendship.

Nat had always been in her life, but childhood sweethearts? She didn't see it as that. Her carefree childhood had terminated abruptly when young Will and Julia had nearly died of diphtheria. Constance had nearly collapsed under the strain and eight-year-old Beth was left to take over the household single-handed until some years later when Aunt

Eva had come to live permanently at Pikesfell Farm.

Will recovered completely, but Julia and Constance remained delicately fragile for a long time. Bernard had been confronted with the thought of life without Constance and now could deny her nothing, so the household revolved round Constance and Julia. Beth's own personality was subordinated and she was content to remain in the background which, given her extrovert siblings, was just as well.

'Possessed by your family,' Nat had said.

She'd never thought of it like that. She loved her family and knew she was one of life's lucky ones in doing so. Eventually the teeming thoughts slowed and she went to sleep.

Daylight, streaming into the room, woke her abruptly. Julia wasn't in bed, nor was Clarice in the corner camp-bed. There was something wrong. The clock showed an unheard of ten o'clock and no-one had woken her. Swiftly she washed and dressed. The house was too quiet, not even a sound from Mrs Earnshaw's kitchen. She ran down the stairs into the dining-room and was greeted by noisy cheering and clapping.

'We thought you'd never get up.'

'Clarice wanted to wake you, but we planned a surprise engagement breakfast.'

Henry seized her and waltzed her round the room.

'Here comes the bride, forty, fat and wide!'

'Congratulations, Sis. Good old Nat, at last!'

'What?'

Beth pulled away as Constance came to hug her.

'We're so pleased. Not surprised, of course. Haven't I always said, Bernard, made for each other, these two?'

'But we're not. I haven't . . . it's a mistake. Where is Nat? What's he said?'

Jim Benson kissed her cheek.

'Nat told me last night. He couldn't contain himself. He's at the hall checking on whether they can muster a few more lights.'

He looked at Beth doubtfully. She didn't look like a girl in love and in the first joyous flush of an engagement.

'What do you mean, a mistake?'

Jubilation died away as Beth sat down and put her head in her hands. Julia poured her a cup of tea.

'Isn't it true, then?' she asked tentatively.

Beth took the cup.

'Not quite as Jim thought. It's true, Nat did speak last night and it was such a surprise. I . . . well . . . I just didn't . . . I'm sure I didn't lead Nat to think . . . '

In different circumstances the disappointed expressions would have made her laugh.

'No wedding?' Clarice asked wrinkling her nose. 'I'd've liked to be a bridesmaid.'

'Nat should have spoken to me first and avoided all this.'

Bernard frowned. Jim looked sheepish.

'Maybe I jumped the gun. Nat were

that excited at getting it off his chest, and so happy, I just assumed . . . '

Beth shook her head.

'I'm sorry. I don't know what else to say, but I can't pretend.'

Constance decided diversionary tactics would best suit the occasion.

'Heavens, look at the time! We need to get rehearsals over this morning. I want to try my new song.'

She put a comforting arm round Beth's shoulders.

'At least you know Nat's feelings, and he's a good young man.'

She clapped her hands.

'Come along, the rest of you. Beth, you stay here and have some breakfast. Take your time, and don't worry.'

She swept the others away, all except Aunt Eva.

'They don't need me there yet,' Eva said to Beth. 'Shall I ask Mrs Earnshaw to boil you an egg?'

'No. I'm not hungry, thanks.'

'You should eat. There's toast, and I'll get fresh tea.'

'That'd be nice. Then I'll go after the others.'

'No, stay put. I can see you've had a bit of a shock.'

'It was so unexpected. I must be an absolute fool.'

'No need to look so tragic. Fresh tea on the way.'

Eva Telford had been part of Beth's life for as long as she could remember although she'd only come to live permanently at Pikesfell Farm when Beth was ten. She'd been a frequent holiday visitor and always brought excitement and exotic presents, visits to be anticipated and treasured. Then all that had suddenly stopped abruptly.

There'd been whispered conversations between the grown-ups. Beth had over-heard, 'Fast past . . . to be expected . . . had to come home to the family and don't we know why?' None of it made any sense to the ten-year-old Beth who was too grateful for Aunt Eva's solid, reassuring presence at Pikesfell to care about the reasons why she was there.

She was glad Eva had stayed behind this morning.

'Auntie, did you ever think Nat and I . . . you know . . . '

She drank the scalding tea gratefully.

'It crossed my mind once or twice but maybe that was wishful thinking.'

'You want me to marry Nat?'

'I want you to marry, have children, your own family, of course I do. You're a talented, young lady with a lot of love to give and I don't want you to end up like me, Miss Spinster Aunt.'

'I've never thought of you like that. You're dear Aunt Eva, and I'm not talented or attractive.'

Eva pursed her lips in disapproval.

'Don't be ridiculous. Without you, your family would have collapsed years ago. Look how you coped when Constance was ill. You've propped them up long enough. It's time to lead your own life.'

'That's just what Nat said.'

'Well, there you are. You could do worse than Nat.'

'So I should accept his offer?'

'My dear girl, you must make up your own mind. Do you love him?'

'I don't know. I never thought about love, never expected it.'

'Good grief, girl,' Eva said, rolling her eyes in exasperation, 'think about it now. Get out from under Constance's and Julia's shadows and, don't take offence, take a bit more trouble about how you look. Stop wearing Julia's cast-offs. They aren't your style, and treat yourself to a good cut and style at the hairdresser's. There, I've spoken out. Now you'll hate me.'

'As if I could. I don't seem to have had time for clothes and hairdos, but you've given me something to think about.'

'Good. Now perhaps we can think about tonight's performance.'

'In a minute. Tell me, why didn't you marry? Weren't you ever in love?'

Eva cast a strange look at her niece, the merest hint of a shadow in her eyes, but she answered lightly.

'Naturally, most people have at least one opportunity in a lifetime.'

'So?'

'Nothing. As you see, I'm Eva Telford, Spinster of Pikesfell.'

'But why? Tell me, there's something, isn't there?'

'Far away down the years and too complicated to think about now. One day perhaps when we're both old and grey — and memory serves.'

She touched Beth's hand.

'Duty calls. One last word about you and Nat. Don't be rushed, make sure you're sure, but don't turn the young man down flat. Give it serious thought.'

'I will,' Beth said simply, 'and thanks, Aunt Eva.'

The Tourers' last venue before Christmas was Grimston. After that the party would split between London and North Yorkshire. Grimston was not a popular date. The school hall was draughty and not centrally located.

'Grim by name, grim by nature,' Will always said.

They never did well there but the Telfords needed the pre-Christmas business to perk up the takings for the London trip. They arrived early afternoon, to bleak streets, grumpy-looking people, and for good measure, stinging rain turned icy with snow and slush.

'Bound to keep everyone indoors tonight,' Will grumbled as they unloaded their luggage.

At least the lodgings were cheerful. A warm welcome, a promise of tea and muffins before a blazing parlour fire guaranteed a good start. Constance settled in a fireside chair and held out her hands to the blaze.

'I knew we shouldn't have come here. Dreary last time, drearier now. Didn't you notice, the streets were deserted?'

'Folk'll be there later,' Bernard said without much conviction, 'and we'll give them a good run for their money.'

'With a long face like that, my love, you'll have them sobbing into their programmes.'

She took his hand and shivered.

'You're so cold. You don't look too well. Sit here by me. Time you had a good rest.'

'I'm fine. I must go to the hall. It was in a poor state last time, no heating, the floors not swept.'

'I'll go, Dad,' Beth offered. 'I've some Christmas shopping to do.'

She wasn't pleased to find the school hall locked with no sign of a caretaker. She waited a freezing half an hour then left a note pinned to the door requesting the heating to be on well before the evening performance. The notice was large, boldly printed and still there when she arrived back an hour before curtain up.

Obviously no-one had been near the place all day. It was dark, deserted and sure to be like an ice-box inside. She'd had trouble with Mr Bates before. She knew he lived a few doors away from the school and now she regretted not going straight there in the first place. Fuming, she rapped on his door. Several raps later a blinking, bleary-eyed caretaker opened the door a crack. She pushed it wider.

'Mr Bates, why aren't you at the school?'

' 'Cos it's the holidays, that's why. Can't a man take a snooze?'

Plus numerous pints of ale, Beth thought grimly, knocked back by the alcohol fumes on his breath.

'We have a booking tonight, the Telford Tourers. You were to have the place opened up and heated.'

'Damned theatricals,' he sneered. 'Boiler's gone out. Can't relight it until after the holidays. Good-night to ye.'

He went to slam the door but Beth was quicker. Her booted foot thrust in the way and she pulled the door right back and stepped over the threshold.

'Mr Bates, if you don't open the school at once and get the boiler going I shall immediately report you to the school board, sue them for breach of contract and you will lose your job. I expect to see you over there in less than five minutes. Clear?'

She turned on her heel and left him cursing all performers.

An hour later, a small, disconsolate audience was sitting wrapped up in as many layers of clothing as possible, jiggling about to keep warm.

'This is terrible,' Constance said as she peered through the thin, worn curtains. 'What a place, and still freezing.'

'The boiler is on now at least, so the warmth will come through soon.'

Beth put another shawl round her mother.

'Dad's sent out for hot, mulled wine all round. Look, there's the man from the inn setting up his stall. Why don't you go out there, Mother, and talk to them?'

'What, be seen before the performance? How unprofessional.'

'Well, make it part of the performance, a special Christmas introduction to the stars! You're the hostess. Oh, go on, Mother, it's the last one before the holiday. Bother being unprofessional.

All of you, go and mingle.'

Beth's brilliant idea saved the evening. The startled audience, initially sullen and inclined to mutiny and to ask for money back, was soon mellowed by hot wine and a mince pie apiece. This unaccustomed generosity was matched by the convivial bonhomie of the performers as they moved about the audience, chatting about the concert to come.

Beth played the piano softly from the stage and proudly watched her family work the audience. Mother had them eating out of her hand as usual and a gaggle of young girls perked up no end at the gallant attentions of Will and Henry. Beth sighed with relief. Perhaps the evening would turn out well after all.

After a second round of wine, some of the audience appeared keen to show off their own party pieces. One old man pulled out a flute and started to accompany Beth. Hastily she turned the pages to a final short piece and it was then she noticed one man in particular who stood out from the rest. Dark-haired, broad-shouldered, tall — there was something about him!

Beth couldn't put a finger on it but there was something very different about him. He looked out of place, yet at the same time comfortably at home in the draughty, old school hall. Now he was leaning forward in his seat to talk to Constance but it was Julia his eyes followed until Constance introduced him, then he took Julia's hand and looked intently into her eyes.

Julia seemed disconcerted and Beth deemed it was time to crash into the final carol to signal the performance opening was overdue. The tall man looked disappointed as Julia smiled and left him to join the others on stage. Frowning, he sat down and studied his programme.

'Amazing,' Beth congratulated the players as they took up stage positions for the hand-bell ringing act. 'A real good start.'

'There are more people in now and

the place is really much warmer,' Constance said as she shrugged off her shawl, 'and that tall dark man, I'm positive I've seen him before. I know, he was at Brenton last month. I remember now because he was standing by the door. I noticed he was different from the others then. I've got it, he must be an admirer. Julia has a follower, I'm sure of it.'

# 3

A relaxed, receptive audience and a holiday break to come inspired the Tourers to a final, rip-roaring performance.

'Talk about turning a disaster into a triumph!' Bernard said proudly.

Will, watching from the wings, took the prompt book from his father.

'You're right, Dad. Ma made 'em cry, you make 'em laugh.'

Bernard had caught the excitement, his tiredness had vanished as he put on his farmer's hat and twitched his hay-making smock into place. He and Jim Benson had developed an unexpected talent for writing comic tales of rural life which Bernard delivered in dead-pan, yokel style. Beth had heard all of them many times but they still made her smile and the dour Grimston audience loved them, applauding at the end of each one.

'Isn't he wonderful?' Constance whispered fondly from the wings. 'He'd do so well on the London stage.'

Beth looked at her mother in astonishment.

'London! You're joking. A London audience would laugh at him, not with him. Whatever put that idea into your head?'

'Oh, nothing, but I've been thinking lately. Beth, what's wrong? What are you looking at?'

'At the back of the hall, under the door. What is it? Oh, no, it's smoke!'

As she spoke a yellow glow shone through the partially-glassed door.

'It's in the entrance, outside the hall.'

A crackle of burning was drowned by audience applause, its attention fixed towards the stage, with no inkling of what was happening behind until Constance screamed out.

'Fire!' she roared.

'The side door's locked,' Beth said in horror, 'from the outside. I checked this afternoon. I went to find Mr Bates, but then I forgot. How can we possibly get out?'

She and Will rushed on to the stage. Bernard had seen the flames but was rooted to the spot, ashen-faced, hand pressed to his side.

'Dad,' Henry pushed him. 'Fire buckets, fire brigade, telephone . . . '

Bernard gasped for breath, and now the audience saw its peril and started to run towards the exit door at the back.

'No, no!' Beth yelled. 'Get the side doors open.'

She jumped down from the stage and ran to head off the panic-stricken rush to exit from where they'd entered. For several nightmare seconds it looked an inevitable catastrophe. Beth saw faces distorted with fear, heard children sob and women scream as everyone fought to find a way out. Smoke swirled more densely, people coughed on the acrid fumes. She tried to fight her way to the side door but bodies were pressed against it, struggling with the lock, banging with their fists.

'It's locked,' she heard a terrible cry. 'We're trapped.'

'Quiet, all of you. Away from the door and stand still. Put handkerchiefs or scarves over your noses. Let me through.'

The voice commanded and was automatically and immediately obeyed. The stranger addressed Beth.

'No other way out?'

'A door backstage, but it's behind a mass of junk.'

'This has to be the way then.'

He turned to the cowering crowd behind him, singling out a dozen hefty-looking chaps.

'Two teams. Use the seating benches as battering rams, aim as near to the centre of the door as you can. We'll soon break the lock.'

'Solid double doors,' Will said. 'We won't shift 'em.'

'No alternative. Get moving, now. When I give the signal charge with all your strength.'

He dropped his arm, the men

charged, the doors shuddered but held.

'Again, faster, harder.'

This time a panel cracked but the lock held.

'One more time, directly at the lock.'

He took a hold on the bench and at the third blow the doors burst open. Men and benches tumbled on to the street, the men gasping in the sweet night air before picking themselves up and instinctively turning back to the burning building to help out families and friends.

'Quickly, all out, and don't crowd the entrance.'

The stranger plunged back into the hall where Beth and Julia were already shepherding people out.

'Where's Mother?' Julia called out.

'I don't . . . look, by the door. There's something wrong with Dad.'

As Beth ran towards the doors a clanging of bells announced the arrival of the fire engine and within seconds firemen were unrolling hoses, connecting fire hydrants and training water jets on to the building. The stranger half-carried Bernard Telford out, Constance close by his side. To Beth's relief her father was protesting loudly.

'I'm all right, thanks, but make sure everyone's out, then the instruments and . . .'

He coughed and gasped for breath.

'He's not well.'

The stranger set him down on one of the benches.

'I'm perfectly well, just a little short of breath,' Bernard said testily. 'Don't fuss, Constance. See to the children.'

Nat and his father carried out boxes from backstage as the firemen brought the blaze under control.

'Beth,' Nat said as he put his arms round her, 'are you all right? What a panic in there. However did that fire start?'

'I can't imagine,' but at that moment she noticed a figure on the edge of the crowd, lingering to watch the firemen. 'Mr Bates,' she called out.

He turned in her direction, cast a

scared look, then vanished into the darkness. Beth made to follow, but Nat held her back.

'Come on, Beth, he wouldn't set fire to his own school.'

'He was furious with me, and drunk. I need to talk to him.'

'Not now. You go back to the lodgings with your mother and sisters. We'll clear up here.'

He steered her towards Constance and Julia who were talking to the tall stranger. Bernard was still sitting on the bench.

'Dad, are you all right? What happened?'

He stood up.

'Just a bit of a turn. Don't you fuss as well. This is Mr Lancaster. His quick action prevented anyone being hurt tonight.'

'What would we have done if you hadn't been in the audience?'

Constance treated Mr Lancaster to a tremulous sigh.

'I expect we'd have managed somehow,' Nat said defensively.

'I'm sure you would.'

The stranger looked at Nat who'd placed his arm protectively around Beth's shoulder.

'My eldest daughter, Beth,' Constance introduced, 'and Nathan Benson, her young man. Mr Lancaster is our saviour of the evening.'

'Please, Mrs Telford, it was no more than self-preservation. I'm only sorry I shan't see the rest of your show, your last before Christmas, you said?'

'Yes, but surely I've seen you before in our audience, at Brenton, last month?'

For a second Angus Lancaster looked disconcerted then adroitly turned it to a look of puzzlement.

'I hardly think so. I was in . . . um . . . London last month.'

'Oh, your double then. Perhaps after Christmas you may catch the rest of the show.'

The man looked at Julia as he answered.

'I should like that. Have you a

handbill with your next venues?'

'Certainly, and please, Mr Lancaster, do join us for supper. Our landlady is putting on a fine supper tonight for our end of season.'

Mr Lancaster hesitated.

'Mr Telford isn't well. It would have been a pleasure but . . . '

'How many more times? I'm right as rain,' Bernard insisted, 'and the least we can do is give you supper.'

'Much as I'd like to, my . . . er, landlady is very strict and has promised supper. Perhaps when we meet again for the second half of the show in another town?'

His eyes lingered on Julia and he raised his hat.

'To our next meeting then, and a happy Christmas to you all.'

The company gathered up their belongings, Constance hovered solicitously around Bernard then placated a few disgruntled members of the audience who wanted their money back. Beth wondered whether she should mention to the police who'd arrived to investigate the fire her suspicions about the caretaker but, as she had no proof, decided there'd been enough excitement for one night. She'd think about it in the morning.

Back at the lodging house, Annie Pilling had done them proud with a seasonal meal of hot goose and roast potatoes. As she served it they speculated on the dark, handsome stranger.

'Something to do with the arts. Theatre, I think. An actor manager perhaps, or an agent looking for talent,' Constance decided.

'Talent,' Will spluttered, 'in Grimston?'

'He was very taken with Julia,' Constance persisted. 'Couldn't take his eyes off her, could he, Beth?'

'I didn't notice,' Beth replied shortly.

'He was handsome though,' Julia sighed. 'I bet he's an important London person.'

'Well, he wouldn't be staying in a lodging house in Grimston, would he?'

Henry said reasonably enough.

Unwittingly, he came nearest the truth. As the Telfords grew merry and mellow over their meal, Angus Lancaster was giving instructions to his driver before settling into Grimston's one and only hotel.

'We'll head back in the morning, Fred. Give it a break until after New Year. Are you comfortable here?' he asked his chauffeur.

'Fine, sir, and I've a cousin in the next town. I'll pay him a visit, see if he knows of anything in the county. Mind you, he's not much of a one for theatricals but his wife's a rare old gossip, knows everyone for miles around. Was there a fire in the town tonight? I thought I heard fire engines.'

'Yes, at the school itself where the Telford Tourers were playing. Nobody hurt, and it was soon under control. Nine sharp in the morning then.'

Fred saluted.

'Nine sharp, Mr Lancaster. Enjoy your dinner.'

'I hope. It'll be good to be home tomorrow and stay put for a few days.'

'Any nearer completing your mission, sir?'

'Not that you'd notice, but I can't give up hope yet. I promised the old man I'd give it a full year and there's still half of it left.'

'Good luck then, sir, and good-night.'

'Good-night, Fred.'

Before he could sample the joys of the Station Hotel's fine dining he made several long-distance phone calls and afterwards went to his room and made a note of the calls and the day's events. Finally he poured himself a whisky and soda from the tray on a side table and sat down to think about the Telfords, cataloguing them in his mind.

Handsome, theatrical Constance was the sun around whom the other stars revolved — Bernard Telford, more farmer than actor, solid, reliable though not in the best of health, older than his wife by a decade; the two boys, typical lads, probably about to break cover into their own lives, and last but not least, the daughters, pretty little Clarice, Betty, no Beth, the backstage stalwart and accompanist with the cross fiancé, and Julia, young, beautiful blonde-haired Julia!

How his heart had missed a beat when he first saw her and then again at Constance's side, wide-eyed and serious, staring at the flames. Then logic had told him how ridiculous it was, sheer coincidence. He flicked through the pages of a notebook, studied a particular photograph intently, then rubbed his eyes and snapped the book shut.

No more tonight, he was tired. Thank goodness, home tomorrow, back to civilisation and comfort.

He went down into the dining-room and cheered up. The smells were encouraging and the service attentive, a satisfactory ending to a difficult day.

Beth woke early next morning with a sense of childish excitement. She was going home to Pikesfell, back to the farm she loved. There was a little pang of regret she wasn't going to London with the others but just now she needed the farm. One thing still niggled in her brain, however, and she had to settle it before she left Grimston. She slipped out of the guest house before the others came down and headed towards the school. To her amazement she saw Mr Bates in the main road, well away from the school. He saw her, stopped, waited and took off his cap.

'Miss Telford,' he said quickly, 'I was coming to see you.'

He was quite sober, shaven, neatly-dressed and looking very frightened.

'About that fire, it weren't my doing. I could see from that look of yours you'd settled on me being to blame. Well, I wouldn't be so foolish. That school's my livelihood. I know I didn't treat you earlier with respect but, well, I haven't been too well. You ain't spoke to the police?'

'No, I haven't. I was coming to speak to you first. How did the fire start?'

'I'm as in the dark as you. I left the boiler properly shut down and anyways it's in the cellar. Fire broke out at the entrance. I swear, miss, it were nowt to do with me.'

Beth considered. He seemed to be telling the truth and she'd no proof and as no-one had been hurt there was little point in pursuing it.

'All right, I'll believe you.'

'And you'll not let on to the school board, about me being . . . uh . . . about the boiler?'

'No, I won't, as it's Christmas.'

'Thank you, miss.'

He grabbed her hand and shook it enthusiastically.

'I can enjoy the festivities with a settled mind. Thankee.'

With another touch to his cap he was off, almost running down the road.

Beth shrugged, but Mr Bates wasn't her problem. As she turned to go back to the lodging house a big black motor car swung round the corner. Cars were still very much a novelty and most passersby stopped to stare. There were two men, the driver, and his passenger in the back, reading a newspaper. In a flash it was off in the London Road direction.

She hurried on. The air was sharp and she was hungry but as she reached Annie Pilling's front door something jolted in her memory. The man behind the newspaper was vaguely familiar. She pondered for a minute or two. The car looked posh enough for a celebrity. She pushed open the gate and forgot all about it, her mind racing ahead to Pikesfell. The next day, at this time, she and Clarice might be on the fells riding Holly and Sunlight, the dogs running alongside. She couldn't wait.

★   ★   ★

The days at Pikesfell passed all too quickly. It was all so wonderfully familiar. The old stone farmhouse, lived in by generations of Telfords, had remained little changed down the centuries. Beth loved its solid comfort, especially the farmhouse kitchen with its vast, old-fashioned range. Uncle Alf and his wife had welcomed the travellers warmly.

It had snowed in the last few days but a bright winter sun in a deep-blue sky had turned the fells into a wonderful winter wonderland and she and Clarice had walked the dogs each day across the dales behind the farm.

But now it was almost over. Constance, Julia and the boys had extended their London stay through to New Year's Eve but were due back for the traditional Pikesfell January First celebrations.

Bernard had taken the trap to the station. Beth and Clarice stayed to help Aunt Mary and Eva with supper. Nat and Jim were also invited. They'd been visiting Nat's mother's family in Lancashire so Beth hadn't seen much of her so-called young man. When he'd kissed her goodbye on Christmas Eve he'd given strong hints they should be planning their future.

'Settled in the New Year,' he'd said.

Beth didn't feel ready to settle anything with Nat just now. She was anxious about her own family's future. She had a sixth sense that there were changes coming and as she and Clarice laid out crackers and napkins in the formal dining-room behind the kitchen she knew the peaceful minutes were numbered and that her mother's arrival would herald the break-up of the quiet days they'd enjoyed.

Still, with Constance back, life was never boring and it was time they livened up again. She'd occasionally thought of Angus Lancaster, wondering if he'd turn up again and if he really was interested in Julia.

Clarice dropped a bundle of crackers on to the table.

'Listen, that's the carriage! They're here, Beth, let's go meet them.'

Beth eagerly followed her excited sister into the hall and laughed at the noise level. The Telfords were together again!

'Hi, sis. You should have come with us, just staggering!'

Will and Henry swung her from one to the other then Julia hugged her, words tumbling like a waterfall.

'London . . . so exciting . . . people . . . motors . . . theatre, music, and the clothes, fashions . . . have to go again soon. Beth, you must . . . '

Then she was off, hugging her father, the aunts, whirling Clarice off her feet, waltzing her round the hall.

'Something every night, and Will's got a young lady.'

'Hey, none of that. You promised,' Will said and turned crimson.

Constance clung to her husband.

'Bernard, you're looking so much better. I knew a rest away from me would do you good.'

'My dear, I've missed you dreadfully. It's Pikesfell's magic, and Mary's good home cooking that's done the trick for me.'

Just then, Nat and Jim arrived and there were more hugs, greetings and talk and chatter until Mary had literally to drive them all into the dining-room for supper, and even then they never stopped talking for a second!

# 4

Afterwards, Beth tried to recall just when the festive mood had soured. Maybe they'd had too much of Mary's home-made elderflower wine, but more likely the tensions were always there under the surface. Early in the meal Beth had sensed her mother was agitated, but excited, too. She'd amused them with her account of sight-seeing, shopping and theatre visits.

'The Mikado was the best show we saw, I think, such gaiety, colourful costumes, a marvellous audience. A wonderful evening, wasn't it, children?'

Julia and the twins nodded agreement as Constance went on.

'So you see, Bernard, London is where we should be.'

'Well, you must go again soon when there's a break in our programme. We've bookings in the South next month,' Bernard said quickly.

'No, not for a holiday. I want us to be based there, permanently. We've done our stint in the provinces. It's time to move on.'

Eva voiced what the others were thinking.

'London? Permanently? What would we do there?'

'Why, perform of course,' Constance said and shook her head impatiently. 'Obviously not in the West End straight away, though Julia might well try for a rôle in one of the productions. She's heaps better than a lot we saw, and we could try places like Camden, Holloway, Hampstead, and in the summer we could fall back on the south coast resorts.'

Bernard banged his hand down on the table.

'Stop, Constance, you're talking nonsense. We're just a small, family group doing very little business in small, provincial towns. Bookings for this year are down and that's a general trend. The new moving picture shows are immensely popular and the wireless is beginning to have an impact, too. There's more entertainment to choose from and we're being edged out.'

'Bernard Telford, you've no ambition, but I have and I'll not see the children's lives moulder away in tin pot draughty school halls.'

'Children!' Bernard exploded. 'Look around! There's only one child, Clarice, and she's growing up fast. Don't they deserve a choice?'

'But they loved London, didn't you?' she asked, her expression daring them to disagree.

'I did,' Julia spoke up loyally.

'I'm not going to London,' Clarice announced.

'And Beth and I will have our own plans,' Nat said.

'What may they be?' Beth turned on him. 'I don't recall any plans mentioned.'

'Because I haven't seen you. I wanted to talk tonight, but now . . . '

His plaintive cry was drowned as voices rose in argument until Eva called out, 'Hush, this is bedlam. No need for a row. Constance has made a proposition. It's a radical one but we should discuss it as we do all matters to do with the Tourers, quietly and rationally.'

Privately Eva thought her sister-in-law had finally gone off her head and a calm, family discussion would soon squash such a daft idea. London was just a fantasy. Bernard took control.

'Eva's right, and I have something to say before this gets any further. I've done some thinking over the holiday. I've walked the farm with Alf and seen how he's swamped with work. I've also watched the colour come back to Clarice's and Beth's faces.'

He cleared his throat and glanced at Constance.

'I've decided I don't want to leave Pikesfell again. The Tourers has been a marvellous family experience I wouldn't have missed but it's over now. Grimston put the lid on it for me and I want to quit. Let this next year be a return to sanity, to Pikesfell and our proper lives.'

Constance went white and her hand fluttered to her lips.

'The Tourers is our proper life. Just as we're moving on you can't suddenly announce it's over!'

'Constance, I'm tired, and ten years older than when we started the venture. I left the farm to follow you on your great adventure because I love you. I could see you were becoming restless and bored here. I couldn't bear to see you unhappy and I thought after a while the travelling theatre bug would die and you'd be happy to settle at Pikesfell. I never reckoned on ten years. Now I want my roots back.'

'You could grow new roots in London. Buy a little house . . . '

'I don't want a little house in London. My house is here.'

There was a profound, prolonged silence. Constance was biting her lip but her colour had returned. She went to her husband and put her arms round his neck and spoke so softly the others hardly heard.

'You've indulged me over the years and perhaps I've taken advantage of that. I know your heart has often longed to be here at Pikesfell and you've resisted that, to please me. I ask one final favour. Give us one more year, to fulfil our contracts and at the same time let me try for some London bookings. One more push for fame and I swear to you, before all the family, if it doesn't work I will come back to Pikesfell and settle happily.'

Again there was silence. Constance's dark eyes bored into her husband's, bending him to her will. Beth knew exactly what her father would say. His shoulder slumped as he spoke slowly.

'You know I can refuse you nothing. If you really are set on this hare-brained scheme I'll go along with you, but for me it will be my last year of travelling and I hope with all my heart that after that you will be with me at Pikesfell, for good.'

Constance kissed him.

'I promise, and thank you.'

Nat's eyes held Beth's, asking her to speak, but she shook her head, not knowing what to make of the bombshell Constance had lobbed into their New Year's celebration. The party ended on a subdued note. The holiday was over and their minds would have to move on to packing up in preparation for their first venues of the new year.

'We'll clear the dishes then maybe try some new songs in the parlour,' Constance said to flag up their spirits.

Beth picked up dirty plates, but Nat took them from her.

'We have to talk.'

'Not now. I must help Aunt Mary.'

'There's plenty others to do that. I expect you did your fair share getting dinner ready. Can't we go somewhere private to talk?' he asked.

'Dad's study. There's a fire in there,' Beth said resignedly, 'but I need to practice the new songs, too.'

'You might not.'

Nat was enigmatic, and once in Bernard's study he took Beth in his arms and kissed her.

'I've missed you,' he said. 'I would have come back sooner but something important happened.'

'What was that?'

'Uncle Stan, he's retiring, and wants me to have the farm, along with Dad if he wants. It's a fine house, a couple of cottages, good land, not far out of the village. You wouldn't be lonely. We can move into a cottage while Uncle Stan finds a house in Scarborough. Auntie Ethel can't wait to go. We can be married next month.'

'Whoa, not so fast, Nat. We haven't decided to marry yet. I did tell you I wasn't sure, and what about the Tourers? You heard Mother. I can't just up and leave them.'

'Why not? What's more important, Beth, your family or us?'

It was difficult. Beth had grown used to thinking of Nat as her young man. He was attractive, she knew he loved her and she liked him kissing her. Was that enough? She remembered Aunt Eva's words and wondered what sort of future she and Nat would have. Up until tonight she thought the Tourers were her future, with Nat tagging along. That was unfair and selfish, and was it fair to let Nat go on hoping she would grow to love him, to marry him?

'Nat, I like you a lot but I've never said I love you. I'm just not sure.'

'You will love me once you're away from your family. They swamp you.'

'That's not true, but I do have an obligation to them, especially now after Dad's ultimatum. Maybe it is the end of the Telford Tourers, and I need to rethink the future, but a year, Nat, that's all I'm asking. We can be properly engaged if you like, then see what happens.'

'But the farm's free now.'

Gently she said, 'Why don't you take the farm yourself? The Tourers was a diversion for you anyway.'

'I came along because I love you,

Beth, and if you're set on another year I'll just have to put up with it. I'll not be away from you for a whole year.'

'But I'd come back in between. There's a whole stretch of time in April when we don't have bookings.'

'Your ma's set on London. She'll be trying for engagements in April.'

Beth sighed. Perhaps Nat was right. Suddenly the thought of a year's travelling appeared unattractive. She'd loved being at Pikesfell this holiday.

'All right, here's a compromise. Let me have six months with the Tourers then I promise I'll know then how I want my life to go. I'm sorry it's unfair on you, but I have to be honest, and anytime you want to leave . . . '

'I won't. I'll be where you are, Beth, that's a certainty. Uncle Stan will just have to wait to retire to Scarborough.'

He held her close and kissed her. Beth responded but didn't know if she was glad or sorry but she had an uneasy feeling the next few months weren't going to be plain sailing.

Throughout a bitter, cold January, the Telfords worked their way southwards. The bad weather kept audiences small, and in poorly-heated rooms Clarice and Julia developed coughs and sore throats. The repertoire had to be adjusted and Constance had little time to look for engagements around London. Will grew increasingly restless and moody as bad roads prevented him from seeing his newly-acquired lady friend in London.

Morale was low and when Aunt Eva was called back to Pikesfell to nurse Aunt Mary through a bad bout of pneumonia it plummetted even lower. Without Aunt Eva's calming diplomacy, tempers frayed and small irritations, laughed off in the old days, became major bones of contention. Beth was more and more certain the Tourers wouldn't last the full year. Father was right — their time had run out.

Nat had bought her a ring and there was a light and hopeful spring in his step as he began to read farming magazines between lulls in performances. Then the month turned and February brought a few days of watery sun. Eastbourne, their next venue, brought them nearer to London and they'd always done good business at the seaside resort. The town was busy on a blustery day of sun and showers as the Telfords arrived at the Assembly Rooms to set up for the evening performance. Constance was in high spirits.

'Things can only get better now, you'll see. Tonight's a sell-out. February, fresh start, all of you remember that.'

The show zipped along and Beth, accompanying her mother, had never heard her sing so well but because the piano was turned away from the audience she didn't know the reason for Constance's inspired performance until they went backstage. Constance was bubbling over with the news.

'He's here, in the audience, third row centre — Angus Lancaster! He's come to see Julia. Bernard, we must invite him back for supper.'

'I can't go down into the audience now. I'll try and catch him at the end.'

'You must, you must.'

After the show, Angus Lancaster strolled along the promenade to give the Telfords time to get back to their rooms. He'd been on his way backstage when Bernard had rushed out, thrust an address in his hand and declared, 'We won't take no for an answer this time. My wife is quite determined you shall have supper with us tonight.'

It had suited his plan well. He'd been in America for a month pursuing his own career and he was anxious to end the quest he had promised to undertake for his grandfather, Phineas Lancaster. The old man hadn't been pleased about the American break but his grandson had stood firm.

'It's vital I take this assignment, Grandfather. I might not get such an opportunity again.'

'Damn foolery,' Phineas had raged. 'You don't need to travel about the world writing stories. What's wrong with the family business here?'

'Not just stories, but journalism, features, news stories. I'm a newspaper correspondent. You know the difference but are just too stubborn to admit it, and as for the business, I'm not interested. It does very well without me. I've no head for finance and Cousin Eric's brilliant at it.'

'I don't trust Eric. He doesn't let me know what's going on. You should be in the office to keep an eye on him and keep me informed. I don't like it when you're away, and what about our investigation?'

'I'll be back in a few weeks, don't fret. There are a few promising leads. Are you really worried about Eric? What's the problem?'

'Can't put my finger on it. He's up to something. I can always tell.'

'We'll talk about it when I get back.'

Well, now he was back. The trip to America had been a great success. Prominent editors had offered him more work than he could handle and old Phineas was still alive as he had known he would be! Phineas Lancaster wasn't going to let go his fragile hold on life until his own story had a conclusion, however unsatisfactory, and he'd entrusted his favourite grandson to seek out that conclusion.

Now, as he studied the address Bernard had given him, a figure caught his attention. It was a woman leaning on the rail staring out over the black ocean and she looked familiar. He approached and raised his hat.

'Miss Telford, isn't it? What are you doing out here?'

Beth turned. Her face in the moonlight had an ethereal, ghostlike beauty which startled him. Her sister, Julia, had the conventional good looks of a pretty blonde but now he saw Beth's beauty was of a different kind, moving and mysterious.

'I was about to set out for your rooms. I'm invited for supper,' he said.

Beth nodded.

'They'll be back now. I had to talk to Nat. He and his father are at different lodgings from us.'

'Nat? Your fiancé?'

'He's . . . well . . . ' Beth started, then stopped.

Why should Mr Lancaster be the least bit interested in the fragile state of her engagement?

'I just needed some air,' she finished lamely.

'Of course, and now you can show me the way to your lodgings.'

He held out his arm. She took it and felt the fine wool of his coat beneath her fingers. Automatically the action drew them closer together as they turned away from the sea and walked towards the town.

In no time, once they arrived, Bernard was carving slices of hot beef on to plates to pass down the table.

'If we'd known you were in Eastbourne we would have had something special for you, Mr Lancaster.'

Constance smiled at him.

'This looks very special, especially the Yorkshire pudding. You're from Yorkshire, I believe. Beth was telling me about Pikesfell on the way here. It sounds a wonderful place,' Angus Lancaster replied.

'It is,' Bernard said, 'and I hope we shall be settled back there this time next year.'

'No more Tourers?' Angus Lancaster said in surprise.

'No.'

Bernard ignored Constance's frown.

'Henry, pour Mr Lancaster some wine.'

'Mother thinks we should try for London,' Henry said as he filled the glasses.

Angus Lancaster looked across to Julia.

'Would you like that? Your singing voice is lovely. With more training . . . '

'How on earth do we ever hope to break into the London circuit? However talented, you need influence to know someone in the theatre world,' Bernard said crossly.

'You forget, I was on the London stage once,' Constance snapped.

'Constance, dear, that was over twenty years ago.'

'I'm sure Mr Lancaster isn't interested in our family affairs,' Beth interrupted quickly. 'He hasn't told us anything about himself. Where do you live?' she asked.

'Actually, London and . . . '

He hesitated. A plan was presenting itself, a plan of such simplicity he wondered why he hadn't thought of it before.

'I have some connections in London's theatre world. I'm not sure how the Tourers would transfer to the London stage as a group but as individuals or part of an already established ensemble . . . or are you determined to keep together?'

'I'm not,' Clarice said as she spied an escape route. 'I want to go back to the farm and so does Dad. Aunt Eva's there already. Dad wants to go and Beth wants to marry Nat, so you see, Mr Lancaster, we're all split up anyway.

You've come at just the right time.'

'I don't want to interfere in family matters and I can't promise anything positive,' Angus said, 'and there is a condition.'

Bernard was bewildered but his natural caution didn't desert him. Angus Lancaster looked at the eager, expectant faces. Only Beth had her head down, seemingly absorbed in the hands in her lap. When she did lift her head her eyes were clouded. Something was making her unhappy and he wondered why her fiancé hadn't joined them for supper. He turned back to his plan.

'I can introduce you to a friend who's very influential in the London theatre world but in return I want to join the Tourers for, say, a month, to begin with. I've a passable voice and can act if necessary.'

He held up his hand, forestalling the barrage of questions.

'You'll just have to take me on trust with no questions asked. And I don't need any payment. Call it an experience I can make use of. Is it a deal?'

Bernard looked at Constance.

'All right,' he said slowly. 'I can't imagine why you'd want to do such a thing but we'll give you a try. With Eva gone we could do with an extra pair of hands. Will, fill up the glasses and we'll drink a toast to Mr Lancaster's experiment.'

Angus suddenly felt light-hearted and looked forward to stepping into his new rôle, and only hoped it would pay off. At worst it could give him material for an interesting feature on the travelling theatre, at best it could yield important information for his search.

He'd report back to Phineas in the morning. At least the notion of his grandson as a strolling player would amuse his grandfather if nothing else.

# 5

Angus Lancaster's impulsive decision to join the Telfords marked an upturn in their fortunes. Bookings were brisk and twice-nightly performances often requested.

It was Angus who had secured their present grand venue, a brand new hotel in a growing suburb of London. It had a purpose-built ballroom-cum-concert hall with all modern facilities and the company had the run of the hotel as guests.

On the last evening, Constance and Bernard watched the second half of the early-evening performance from the wings. Angus's journalistic talent had taken a surprising turn. He'd written a twenty-minute melodrama in which he and Julia took the leading rôles as a pair of ill-fated lovers. The sketch was in full swing, the audience was enthralled, the only sounds tearful sniffs as the lovers battled against life's dramas and parental disapproval.

'Aren't they both magnificent?' Constance breathed, clutching her husband's arm. 'Julia is so pitiful as the poor, wronged Sophie. She brings a lump to my throat.'

'But you've seen it a score of times so you know the ending. And it's only a tale Angus has made up.'

'But Sir Frank throws her out, disowns her . . . and the baby!'

'Come on, Constance,' Bernard said, who'd had had enough of the melodrama, 'if you're going to get so worked up over Love's Tragedy I'll withdraw it from the repertoire. I'll not have my beautiful leading lady suffering. You've two more songs and another show at half past eight so I'm ordering a cup of tea and a lie down right away.'

'All right, Bernard, dear, I hear you, but don't they make a handsome couple, on and off stage?'

'Handsome as snowdrops in winter,'

Bernard returned enigmatically.

He had a store of such sayings, often unfathomable but appropriate!

'Your ma really lives that awful sketch,' Nat said as he and Beth stood by to bring down the curtain and see on the next act.

'No need to sneer. Angus's sketch is very popular. Just listen to that applause. Open the curtains quick. There's another bow.'

But somehow the curtain ropes were tangled and Nat only managed to straighten them as the applause died away.

'Ah, well,' he shrugged, 'Let's get on to the next act.'

Beth looked at him darkly.

'If I didn't now you better, Nathan, I'd think you did that on purpose.'

Nat was absorbed in checking a faulty light and didn't reply. Flushed and laughing, Angus and Julia came off the stage, arm in arm.

'Wonderful,' Angus said. 'Not a dry eye anywhere and even those tough-looking soldiers were sniffing.'

'Nasty time of the year for hay fever,' Nat commented.

'Nat!' Beth exclaimed. 'The Telford Trio's on stage and Dad's front stage to do the intro. Get the curtain up, unless it's stuck again, of course.'

Julia's smile faded at Beth's sharp tone.

'What's the matter with you two? Had a row?'

'No,' Beth replied. 'My fault, I'm a bit tired. I miss Aunt Eva and . . . '

'It's been a busy few weeks,' Angus said and put his arm around Julia's waist, 'but it's been fun, too.'

She leaned against him.

'Your play is the best hit we've had. You're such a good writer, Angus. You could make your living at it.'

Beth was looking at him with eyes as expressive as her sister's.

'I reckon you could make a living on the stage, too, as actor or singer.'

'I harmonise well with your mother and that's as far as it goes.'

Mentally he gave himself a shake. He

was getting far too enmeshed in these theatricals. It was time he finished the task Phineas had set for him, either resolve it or forget it. He must get back to his real work.

Angus led Julia away towards the dressing-room, bending his head to hers. Beth heard him say, 'Not yet, soon. I expect to hear later in the evening.'

The trio was in full swing. Nat looked at his watch.

'Five minutes to go. Beth, I have to talk to you.'

She had her head down in the prompt book and now put her fingers to her lips, following every word of the duet Clarrie and Will were singing, accompanied by Henry on accordion.

'Not now,' she whispered. 'You're in such a bad mood anyway.'

'Not surprising,' he muttered. 'I'm not part of the Angus Lancaster admiration society.'

A burst of cheering cued the finale of the trio and he swished the now perfectly working curtains together with some ferocity. Nat's mood wasn't improved by the rapturous reception given to Angus's first solo item from The Mikado, music high on Constance's priority since her London trip.

The early-evening show ended with a Gilbert and Sullivan selection specially arranged by Constance for the entire company. Before the second performance, there was an hour's rest for everyone. Nat caught Beth as she was slipping out of the stage door.

'Nat! I was just going for a breath of air. It's a lovely evening. There's a park nearby, I'll just . . . '

He gave her arm a shake.

'Don't try and put me off. You've been avoiding me for days.'

'Surely not. We've been so busy, lots of bookings, new music to learn, and with Aunt Eva away . . . '

'Let's go to the park then. At least there shouldn't be Telfords crawling all over the place in there, or Angus Lancaster for that matter.'

The park was green, quiet and deserted, the setting sun gilding the small bandstand in the middle.

'That's nice,' Beth started. 'Families can come, listen at weekends and holidays. What's Angus Lancaster to do with anything by the way?'

Nat drew her down beside him on an ornate iron seat.

'Since he came, nothing's been the same. He's . . . well . . . he's taken over and you've avoided me.'

'Nonsense. He's new to it and we've all had to spend time with him. You must admit he's improved the show no end. You mustn't be . . . '

She stopped, overwhelmed by guilt because it was true. She had been avoiding Nat because she knew what he wanted. Uncle Stan had written most weeks. He'd found the dream house in Scarborough and was pressing Nat for a decision on the farm. It was time Nat came home, bringing his bride with him. Touring theatricals was no life for a young woman and Beth's place was on Nat's farm, having family to hand on the tradition of farming. Beth had heard Uncle Stan's views on a woman's place in society lots of times.

'Jealous?' Nat said as he picked up her thought. 'Of course I am. You all hang on his every word, run around after him.'

'That's not fair, and gracious me, can't you see it's Julia he's interested in, not me?'

'But you like him. No good denying it.'

' 'Course I like him, and so should you. He's different, and look how business has improved. Nat, don't be so sour about it. It's not like you.'

'You don't really know me, Beth, because your family's always in the way. I want us to be man and wife, have our own family. All this play acting is nonsense, a game, fun for a while but it's not real. It's make-believe! The farm in Yorkshire, that's our life, that's real. I can't stand this any more.'

'You promised, Nat, six months, and

it's only been three.'

Her voice was anguished because in her heart she recognised he was right. Before Christmas she'd realised the Tourers' life was a game, sponsored by Constance. Life at the farm had been lovely and she'd almost decided it was what she wanted but somehow back on the road it was exciting again, an adventure, especially since . . . She shut that thought away. Angus joining them was incidental.

'A while longer,' she pleaded, 'or maybe you should go back, start up at the farm. I could join you later.'

'No, when six months is up it'll be just a while longer again, you'll say.'

'No, Dad said a year. It will end then.'

'Your mother come back to Pikesfell? I doubt it.'

'No-one knows. The future's so uncertain.'

'No. That's the point, ours isn't. Our future's settled, mapped out. You have to decide, Beth, right now, tonight.'

'I can't. I can't leave them.'

'You can.'

Nat stood up and faced her, shadowy now as dusk invaded the park.

'If you want it, our future's there. Take it, Beth. See the week out, then there's a break in the schedule. They'll manage without us and we can go back to where we belong.'

They faced each other, like dark statues. Gas lamps came on in the town beyond and a figure came hurrying towards them out of the dark trees, saw them, slowed and stopped. Beth shuddered.

'I can't, Nat. Don't make me. Not yet.'

His hand dropped, his body sagged. Peering at her he imprinted her face on his memory then kissed her on the cheek.

'I think I always knew in my heart it was too good to be true. You've never loved me, so best if we part.'

He turned and walked away rapidly. Beth knew he wouldn't be back.

'Nat, please, don't go. Please,' she

called out again but the darkness had swallowed him leaving her alone until Angus Lancaster moved swiftly to her side and took her arm.

'Beth, what are you doing? Performance in ten minutes. They sent me to look for you. There's a full house, and wasn't that Nat, your young man? Have you quarrelled? Here, take my handkerchief. Don't cry, he'll be back.'

'He won't, and I'm not crying. I don't . . . oh, let's just get back to the theatre.'

In spite of backstage tensions the late performance zipped along. Nat had simply announced this would be his final performance with the Tourers, saying he had business at Uncle Stan's farm. And so Nat closed the final curtain, then disappeared.

A few of the Tourers had much appetite for the late, light supper the hotel provided. Constance, Julia and Clarrie went early to bed, Bernard went to look for Jim while the twins' business in town was apparently secret and not open to family discussion. Beth was restlessly wide awake and ravenously hungry. Angus kept her company in the deserted hotel dining-room. He looked at her with concern.

'Are you all right? I'm sorry you and Nat have quarrelled.'

'It's not your business,' she retorted.

'You're right, it isn't, but you seemed so . . .'

'I'm fine,' she interrupted, 'and I didn't mean to be rude. That came out all wrong. I meant I don't want to think or talk about Nat just now.'

'I understand.'

'Do you?'

She eyed him curiously.

'You know all about us, the Telford family history. Mother's made sure of that but we know nothing about you except that you work in London and know theatre people. For instance, are you married?' she plunged, thinking that a man as attractive as Angus must surely have some romantic involvement.

He laughed.

'Gracious, no. I've never been in one place long enough.'

'Why's that?'

Beth poured tea from the fresh pot that had swiftly arrived at a gesture from Angus. She was relieved to hear of his bachelor state, otherwise his interest in Julia would be suspect.

'I travel a lot.'

'Doing what?' she persisted.

'Oh, this and that. Projects,' he answered vaguely.

'Theatre connections perhaps?'

'Not exactly.'

He tried to avoid her clear brown-eyed gaze. Difficult to evade, was this girl's questioning. He spoke quickly, anxious to shift the thrust of her curiosity.

'I do have an interest in the theatre, purely as a patron, you understand, and as a matter of fact, I do have a slight personal interest in touring players, too. A distant relative was once connected with a group of performers so maybe there's a little theatre blood in the Lancasters.'

'Really? How interesting. Which group? Where?'

'Bit of a mystery. He, the young man, disappeared some twenty years ago, probably dead now. The family often wondered what became of him. Do you have contacts with other companies? Any friends there?'

'Not really. More rivalry than friendship. Dad would know more than me. Some groups can be obstructive, aggressive, too, if we end up in the same town, although we try not to. There's a lot of competition for venues and we've had a bit of trouble in the past but mostly we're regarded as a bunch of harmless amateurs, until now that is.'

'Why now?'

'You can't have failed to notice how things have improved since you joined us. Word travels fast in this business. We'll have to watch our backs.'

Suddenly a wave of fatigue swept through her, reaction to Nat's departure and the long, working day. She tried to stifle a yawn. Angus got to his feet.

'You're tired, Beth. I've kept you up.'

'No, it's helped, just talking.'

She picked up her bag.

'I've just thought, if you do want to trace your missing boy there's the Players' Broadsheet. It carries news and views of the whole business of travelling entertainers, and there's a huge missing person's section. I'll dig out a copy tomorrow. Worth a try.'

'Indeed.'

Angus had actually advertised in countless papers for news of the lost Lancaster, alive or dead, but had never heard of the Players' Broadsheet.

'Incidentally, I've had news from London, a message that came after the others had gone to bed. My London contact would like to meet the Telfords and he's particularly keen to audition Julia. I'll tell her first thing in the morning.'

'That's wonderful. She'll be thrilled,' Beth said, tiredly noticing how his expression changed when he spoke her sister's name.

# 6

Angus didn't stay at the hotel with the others. He'd returned with some relief to his apartment in Kensington, delighting in its comforts for a few days, nor had he visited his grandfather yet. There was a gap in the Tourers' schedule after their present venue, so that would be time enough then.

The next morning he joined the Telfords in their hotel dining-room, picking up a special delivery letter for Bernard at Reception. Angus's news was greeted with universal appreciation.

'London! An audition!' Constance exclaimed. 'Julia, I'm so proud of you, and the timing's perfect because we've a few days before the Worthing engagement. Bernard, you must book a hotel at once.' She faltered, seeing his serious look. 'Who's the other letter from?'

'Eva, and it's bad news. Mary's had to go back to hospital and Alf's had an accident. Start packing at once. I'll check the train time-table. We'll leave the carriage and the hotel can stable the horses.'

Constance looked up from reading the letter.

'Poor Mary, and Alf, too. How on earth did he come to drive a pitchfork through his foot?'

'Because he's too much to do. I should never have left Pikesfell in the New Year. There's far too much work for one man. This settles it.'

Constance looked alarmed.

'But, dear, London, Julia's audition. Surely it's not necessary for us all to go home. Perhaps the boys, Beth or Clarrie.'

'Your place is with me, Constance. Eva's borne the burden long enough. It's our turn.'

'But for Julia, it's such an opportunity.'

Constance's voice had a note of

desperation. This was a new, commanding Bernard, one she had rarely, if ever, seen.

'Must we all go?' she repeated.

'I want to,' Clarrie spoke up. 'I'd love to go back to Pikesfell, and I can help, too.'

Bernard looked round the table at his family and saw that they were all individuals now, wanting to make their own choices. The group, Telford Tourers, was no longer the priority, which was how it should be and what he'd clearly seen coming during the last year. He considered his position carefully before he spoke.

'You're right, Constance, Julia must have her chance and go to London for the audition Angus has so kindly arranged.'

'Good. I'll stay with her.'

'No. Mary and Eva need both of us. It's time to consider others, dear. London won't disappear, and Beth can stay on with Julia.'

'But they must have a chaperone.

Two young girls can't stay in London on their own.'

'Mother!' Julia and Beth protested in unison.

'We'll stay,' the twins chorused.

'No. You'll be needed on the farm.'

Their faces fell, particularly Will's who saw his chances of spending time with his girl friend, Clara, in London fast receding. He looked mutinous. Bernard knew it was probably the last time he could command his sons.

'Please, boys, we do need you at Pikesfell.'

'Oh, all right then, just for a few days,' Henry answered for both and Bernard sighed with relief.

Angus had been following the family's reactions.

'If you agree, Bernard, I can keep an eye on Beth and Julia. I'll be taking Julia to her audition anyway and I'll be pleased to show the girls some London attractions in between. Alternatively, we could postpone the audition but I should tell you Julia might not get another chance like this. The rôle my friend has in mind has to be cast almost immediately. The original actress fell ill. Bad for her, we hope good for Julia.'

Julia's eyes widened.

'Dad, please?'

Bernard looked from her to Angus and nodded.

'Thank you, Angus. We'd appreciate that. It's settled then. Julia and Beth go to London with Angus, the rest head for Pikesfell, and right now.'

Constance scanned his face and knew there was no reprieve. However, she ventured one last throw.

'We open in Worthing the week after this.'

'We'll cross that bridge when we come to it, my dear. If we have to cancel then I shall cancel.'

Constance noted the determination in her husband with a faint tremor of foreboding, then obediently went to pack.

★  ★  ★

'Can you believe we're here?'

Julia danced round the hotel bedroom high on anticipation and freedom.

'In London, on our own. Wonderful!'

'Aren't you nervous?'

Beth hauled their cases on to the bed and started to unpack.

'Nervous? About the audition? A bit, but that's tomorrow afternoon so I'll think about that tomorrow. Tonight we're going out with Angus to a show, maybe supper afterwards. Isn't it thrilling? I love London. I'm just scared I'll have to go back to Pikesfell for the rest of my life.'

'Would that be so terrible?'

Julia pulled a face.

'Not terrible. It's my home, but it's for when I'm old. I want to do something first, be a somebody, a famous actress.'

Beth watched her sister fondly. How different they were. Her own nerves were jangling already in anticipation of Julia's coming ordeal tomorrow. But then, Julia was Constance's daughter and how Constance would have loved the chance even for an audition on a London stage.

'Don't set too much store by tomorrow,' she felt obliged to warn.

'Don't worry. I trust Angus. If I don't get this one he'll fix another.'

'My, what confidence in Mr Lancaster,' Beth mocked, but in her heart she agreed. 'You like him, don't you?'

'Of course. I love him. Now, what shall I wear tonight? You should try that lovely new jade-green suit Aunt Eva helped you choose, not that old grey silk thing. I can't think why you haven't thrown that out years ago.'

'It's familiar, like an old friend, I suppose.'

But she was glad she'd finally chosen the new outfit when she saw the smart crowd in the foyer of the Palace Theatre, and when she saw Angus, head and shoulders above the rest, her stomach gave a funny half-somersault. Julia positively glowed as he came to greet them. Undoubtedly he was the most attractive man in the crowd.

'How well you both look. I can see London suits you, and you fit in perfectly. The play starts in ten minutes. Shall we find our seats?'

A Telford on each arm, Angus made his way towards the auditorium, noting the admiring looks the girls were receiving. Julia was particularly radiant and very aware, much to Angus's amusement, of the interest she was rousing. The new face on the scene, he murmured to himself. It augured well for her future in theatreland. On the other hand, Beth hung back, more nervous of the smart crowd.

'You look lovely, Beth,' Angus encouraged. 'Your hair's different and it suits you.'

'Thank you. I promised Aunt Eva I'd have it styled and I only got round to it today. Terrible prices they charge in London.'

'Well worth it, whatever. Oh, no.'

He broke off as a loud voice rasped through the genteel buzz of conversation around them.

'Angus Lancaster! Thought you'd left the country. Hoped so after that piece about me in The Times. Ah, see you've been busy. Do introduce me to these exquisite, young creatures. Haven't seen these two before.'

'Lord Bathhurst, I hope you're well. Forgive me but there's the bell and we haven't found our seats yet.'

'Hey, later then, drinks at the interval?'

But Angus had already bustled the girls through a door, out of sight and sound of the braying lord.

'A box! How did you know I've longed to see a show from a box like this? It's . . . it's sumptuous,' Julia exclaimed.

Impulsively, she flung her arms round Angus's neck and kissed him. Beth saw how he held her close for a second before releasing her to take their seats as the orchestra struck up the overture. Beth leaned forward to watch the audience below, a very different crowd from the Tourers' usual audience. The men and women in the stalls exuded wealth. Jewels sparkled at throats and wrists. Several people scanning the boxes waved towards them until Angus moved his seat back into the shadows.

The show was a play interspersed with songs and dances. It was pleasant and undemanding and in the frequent intervals champagne and light refreshments were served in their box. Angus apparently was disinclined to mingle with the fashionable crowd outside and Beth wondered if he was ashamed of herself and Julia in front of his smart friends. Again she wondered, where did he live, what did he do for a living? Would he take them to his house during their stay?

At the end of the performance Angus seemed distracted and as soon as the final curtain call was over he went and hailed a cab, handing them in quickly.

'I'll call for you tomorrow at your hotel. It's late and Julia should rest.'

'Thank you for . . . ' Beth began, but Angus was gone, and as she looked back she saw he was surrounded by a group of people.

She watched them all move off and burst out, 'He's ashamed of us.'

'Ashamed! You do talk nonsense sometimes, Beth.' Julia sighed happily. 'I loved it tonight.'

'I thought we were going out to supper.'

'We had supper. All that champagne! I couldn't eat a thing. Don't be such a cross bear.'

Next day Beth felt thoroughly ashamed of her grumpiness. Of course Angus had friends in London and was anxious to see them after weeks in the wilderness with the Tourers. He'd been immensely kind and when he picked them up late that afternoon she could hardly look him in the eyes.

He was brisk, his mind on a thousand matters, picking up the threads of his real life, a life which seemed somehow unreal after his weeks on the road with the Telfords. He looked at the two girls, Julia looking so vivaciously pretty, he was sure Thomas Brinton would fall in love with her and immediately give her a part in his new musical play. Beth looked tired and he guessed she must be brooding over that young man who'd been foolish enough to leave her. The cab pulled up in a dingy side street.

'Here we are. Not so grand as last night. You'll see the other side of the theatre here.'

'That's the one we're used to,' Beth reminded him.

'It's not really like the Telford Tourers,' she whispered to Angus half an hour later sitting next to him at the back of the stalls watching Julia going through her paces. 'It's much more nerve-wracking.'

'Julia's not a bit nervous. She's doing fine, can't you see that?'

He took her hand and squeezed it reassuringly.

'Don't worry, this is the beginning of great things for your sister.'

Beth let her hand stay in his as she held her breath for Julia.

Two hours later they were back on the crowded London streets, hardly daring to voice their thoughts. Angus sensed they were stunned.

'There's a café down the road. I think you need hot, sweet tea.'

'That's what they give for shock,' Beth stuttered.

'Seems to me you've had a shock. I can't think why because it's no surprise to me.'

The tea-room was crowded with women in elegant hats and smart costumes, several with tiny dogs on their laps.

'Gracious,' Beth exclaimed.

'More shocks?' Angus asked as he poured the tea.

'Not really, it's all a bit overwhelming but, dear Julia, congratulations! You were just amazing.'

'Told you Brinton would find you irresistible. You have real talent, Julia,' Angus said proudly.

'But the London stage. I didn't really think the first time . . . Angus, how can I thank you?'

'No need. But Bernard and Constance should know. Shall I telegraph them?'

Julia's hand flew to her mouth.

'How selfish of me. I was so excited I accepted Mr Brinton's offer straight away without giving the Tourers a thought. That's terrible. Beth, what should I do?'

'Go ahead, of course. We'll talk to them tonight, but a telegram would be a good idea, Angus, a sort of warning. Give them time to think.'

'Mr Brinton wants to start rehearsals next week. Where shall I live, and what about Worthing? How can I abandon the Tourers? Have I made a dreadful mistake?' Julia went on.

'No, you haven't,' Beth said firmly. 'I'm sure Angus will advise us about lodgings.'

'Of course I will, but tonight I'm taking you out to dinner to celebrate. I'm afraid I was rather preoccupied with other matters last night. I'll pick you up at seven o'clock.'

Beth recognised the car immediately as the one she'd seen the very first time they had encountered Angus and she had seen it drive past her in the street, although it had been chauffeur driven before. She realised now it had been Angus in the back, a rich man who hadn't spent the night in a cheap lodging house in Grimston last Christmas. Not for the first time she wondered what Angus Lancaster was up to. Clearly he was not quite what he appeared although, to be fair, he'd never pretended to be poor.

'It's very smart,' Julia whispered to Beth as they were ushered deferentially into the dining-room of one of London's top hotels where Angus was obviously a regular and valued customer.

At the end of the meal, Julia sat back with a contented sigh.

'Pinch me, Beth, perhaps I'll wake up. Today can't be real.'

'It's no dream,' Angus said and signalled the waiter for coffee, 'and it'll be a hard grind once rehearsals start. Now, where would you like to go next? We can dance, see a late show. It's early yet for London.'

'We should be getting back,' Beth said reluctantly. 'Julia must be tired.'

'No, I'm not, it's been such an exciting day, but I would like to go back to the hotel and read the playscript Mr Brinton gave me.'

'Beth?' Angus asked.

'Er — I'm not tired. I'd like a walk, get some fresh air.'

'You'll not find London air as fresh as Pikesfell's but I'm more than happy to walk with you. We'll have a look at the river. Will you come, too, Julia?'

She shook her head.

'I was never one for the great outdoors, like Beth.'

'London will suit you then.'

'I'm beginning to think it will.'

Julia smiled at him.

Having taken Julia back to the hotel Angus took Beth's arm as they walked along the Embankment. It was a warm night, a bright moon silvered the Thames and couples strolled arm in arm, some closely entwined, some locked in close embrace. Beth stopped to lean over the stone parapet.

'It's lovely in its own way, the river. Just imagine what it's seen through the centuries, such changes.'

Angus leaned with her and stood shoulder-to-shoulder.

'It does put our small lives in perspective.'

'We should live them to the full though, shouldn't we?' she said and turned to face him. 'Julia's life will change. I can't imagine life without her.'

'She's only changing direction, not disappearing.'

'Will you be seeing her in London when you've finished with the Tourers?'

'Of course, when I'm here. I feel responsible for her.'

'Do you? I'm glad.'

Her face, turned to his, had that same slightly sad, ethereal quality he'd seen before as she'd watched the sea at Brighton. She was beautiful, with a beauty Angus found intensely moving. At that moment it seemed the two of them existed alone in their moonlit world by the Thames, their faces so close it was inevitable for Angus to turn her to him and kiss her.

There was a second of startled surprise as his lips touched hers, then an unknown, unexpected fire coursed through her body, her own lips yielding to his, a sensation she wanted to hold for ever, but a mournful hoot of a barge downriver startled them apart.

Their eyes locked. Beth was the first to look away, her breathing uneven, her heart pounding.

'I . . . I . . . ' she began to say, but Angus put his finger over her lips.

'Don't. I'm sorry, Beth, that was unforgiveable but you . . . forget it happened, please. I'll take you back to the hotel.'

'How can I forget!' a silent voice cried in her heart. 'I don't want to.'

In silence, they walked back to the hotel, not touching, formal, polite.

'That shouldn't have happened, Beth,' he said as they stood by the hotel steps. 'I hope it won't spoil our friendship. For a moment I forgot you're engaged to Nat.'

'I . . . '

But with a brief handshake he was gone, striding quickly in the direction of his grandfather's house, resolving once again to bring the search for the missing Lancaster heir to its obvious conclusion. The boy was surely dead, and Angus had no more time to spend on the wild-goose chase of searching for him, cousin or not, a search which was proving far too distracting.

# 7

Martha Clarke, Phineas's housekeeper ever since Angus could remember, greeted him like a traveller returned from wild and distant parts.

'What a relief to see you. Your grandfather isn't well. Mr Eric's here now, in the study, pestering him again.'

'How long's he been here?'

'An hour or so. He knows what's going on. I didn't say a word.'

'I know that, Martha. Eric has a way of ferreting things out.'

Outside the study door Angus grimaced as he heard Eric's loud, hectoring voice, but he was shocked to see how frail his grandfather looked.

'Angus,' the old man's face lit up as he spoke, 'at last. Where've you been? We've heard some odd rumours.'

'I told you I'd attached myself to a group of travelling entertainers.'

'Eric here says you've joined a gipsy band.'

He acknowledged his cousin with a brief handshake.

'Why do you upset Grandfather with such rubbish?'

Eric Lancaster, a florid, young man a couple of years older than Angus, turned on him.

'It's what I heard and now I think I know why. It's not for one of your newspaper articles, is it?'

'I'm sorry, Angus,' Phineas said. 'He pestered and pestered until he got it out of me.'

'Bullied you, more like.'

Angus glared at his cousin feeling the usual prickle of years of antagonism between them.

Phineas Lancaster was a self-made man of great wealth, moving as a young man from his native Scotland to develop his business interests in London. He had the Midas touch for money but his family life was ruined by tragedy. His two sons and their wives had been killed in a boating accident, orphaning both young cousins, Angus and Eric.

Phineas and his wife, Eliza, reared the boys as best they could but Eric was a difficult child and Phineas finally packed him off to boarding school for which Eric never forgave him. Eric then went into the family business, Angus into journalism. They never got on, but for their grandparents' sake managed a semblance of family unity which held just so long as they didn't meet too often. Tonight looked like a testing point for that precarious unity.

'So what's the problem, Eric?' Angus spoke calmly.

'The problem is that you've excluded me from any knowledge of this ridiculous mission to find our long-lost cousin, a boy I never knew existed until recently. I am family, or has it escaped your notice?'

'There wasn't a lot of point in telling you until there was some news. I didn't know the full story until Grandfather asked me to search for Albert.'

'And what if you do find him?'

'That's up to Phineas.'

They both turned to the old man whose hands were trembling violently.

'You don't have to go on, you know,' Angus said gently.

'I do, I do. I have to find Mary's boy, atone for my terrible sin. My own child, pretty, little Mary. After our sons, your fathers, were killed, Eliza and I set such store by our last child, Mary. We spoiled her most likely, everybody did, especially after the ... the yachting accident.'

'She was pregnant and you turned her out,' Eric stated baldly.

'I did, to my shame, but she was stubborn, wilful, refused to consider adoption, wouldn't name the father. I thought she'd come to her senses but she left the house seven months into her pregnancy, taking nothing but what she was wearing. I was so hurt and angry I forbade any mention of her, disowned her, wiped her from my memory, except I couldn't . . . can't . . . '

'But she died,' Eric said brusquely, 'so why bother now?'

'But the child didn't.'

'How do you know?'

'Because, Eliza, your grandmother, secretly kept in touch with Mary and the boy. She tried to tell me once or twice but I wouldn't listen. Can't you see, the pair of you, why I have to find him?'

'There's so little to go on,' Angus said. 'Just scraps Grandmother told Martha before she died.'

'Martha was Eliza's maid. She trusted her, and when Martha saw recently how determined I was to find the boy she told me every word Eliza spoke.'

There was a profound silence before Angus said slowly, 'And what she wrote down was, 'Mary will forgive . . . the baby, Albert . . . entertainers . . . North of England.' The only clear words in a jumble of incoherence was about dancing, singing and circus performers.

I know the boy is alive and I intend to give him his inheritance,' Phineas said slowly, 'for Mary's sake.'

'Inheritance?'

Eric's voice was thunderous.

'What inheritance? If he's alive, which I doubt, he doesn't deserve anything. It's our money you're giving away. It'll cost a fortune in legal fees. It's sheer stupidity. You have to forget it. I'm going to put a stop to this absurdity.'

'Eric, for goodness' sake, can't you see Grandfather's ill? He can't breathe. Call Martha.'

'I'm here.'

She moved to Phineas, loosening his collar, rubbing his hands.

'He's upset. I heard you shouting, Mr Eric. Now, please call the doctor at once. Mr Angus, help me get him to bed. Go on,' she said to Eric, 'you've caused enough damage. Shift yourself and get help.'

Phineas had suffered a mild stroke which improved after a few days' rest.

With a feeling that time was running out he urged Angus to continue his search, sparing no expense. Accordingly Angus hired new investigators and widened the net of newspaper advertisements, including the Players' Broadsheet as well as every other theatrical magazine and newsheet.

He decided to return to the tourers in Worthing for a final few weeks but before he left he settled Julia in a comfortable and homely lodging, sharing with a couple of other girls from the show. Julia was apprehensive, a little homesick for her family, and very excited. At her new lodgings she said goodbye to Angus, standing on tip-toe to kiss him.

He looked at her intently and felt again that curious jolt of recognition, as of a memory imprinted long ago. He hugged her and returned her kiss.

In Worthing, Angus found the atmosphere gloomy, with a sense of malaise hanging over the company. Eva was back but Bernard worried dreadfully about Alf coping alone with the farm and a poorly wife. Clarrie pined increasingly for Pikesfell and they all missed Julia. Constance, too, had lost some sparkle, her heart in London.

Audiences were small and after the first couple of performances there was heckling and drunken shouting, so much so that Bernard felt it was wise to cut the last items to prevent any trouble.

'Eastbourne will be better,' Eva promised, 'a much better place.'

But it wasn't. There was more heckling, even booing from a noisy minority. Bernard cancelled the second half of the show and returned ticket money to a disgruntled audience. It was bad publicity and there were few ticket sales for the rest of the week.

'Something odd's going on,' Bernard told his Tourers. 'Someone is trying to wreck our show, frightening off our regulars.'

'A rival company?' Angus guessed.

'Possibly. We've done so well lately

we're a threat to the competition. It's beyond me.'

The twins exchanged glances, imperceptible nods, and stood up.

'If it's all right, Dad, Will and I have some business in town.'

'All right, but be sure you're back before eight. A good house tonight for once. Fingers crossed.'

'Stacks of time,' the twins echoed and left.

Bernard went to check the stage with Jim. He missed Nat's strong young presence, too. He worked on before suddenly realising the time.

'Eight o'clock, it is, and no twins,' he observed.

'They'll be here,' Eva said confidently as she joined him backstage.

Eight thirty came, a quarter of an hour before curtain up. Angus went out to look for them. He came back looking grim.

'Nowhere in sight, but there's been some trouble in the town. Police are everywhere. A fight in a pub, apparently, and several hurt.'

'You don't think Will and Henry were involved?' Constance said fearfully.

'There's a policeman in the hall,' Jim announced as he twitched the curtains. 'Looks official.'

Beth was very worried.

'Mr Telford?' the policeman asked who climbed on to the stage.

The audience buzzed expectantly, impatience momentarily forgotten in the possibility of a real-life drama.

'What is it?'

Bernard put his arm round Constance.

'I'm afraid there's been an accident, several people in hospital. Don't worry. Is this Mrs Telford? Your lads aren't too bad.'

He consulted his notebook.

'Henry and William Telford? A bit knocked about. One lad's broke an arm, the other a toe, and a bloody nose. Both in hospital doing well.'

He stopped in alarm as Constance sank back to her chair.

'I should look to Mrs Telford,' he

advised unnecessarily, 'and that lot out there are getting restless. Best cancel the performance, I'd say. Those lads of yours won't be performing tonight.'

At that Constance suddenly sat up.

'I'm perfectly all right,' she announced. 'And of course we're performing tonight. We have plenty to spare in our repertoire without the boys. Thank you, constable. We will visit them after the show. If you'll excuse us now.'

Beth, Clarrie and Angus walked back after the performance through the quiet streets of the town. Bernard had taken Constance to the hospital straight after the final curtain.

'Your mother is remarkable,' Angus said. 'She has a real talent for turning disaster into triumph.'

'She's done it before. Trouble brings out her fighting spirit.'

'The audience lapped it up. You and Clarrie were pretty good, too.'

The girls shrugged modestly.

The twins returned the next day, patched up, unchastened and unrepentant.

'We had to do it, Dad,' Will said. 'That gang was responsible for the trouble we've had, 'specially primed to disrupt. One of them boasted about it before I knocked him out. We beat the lot of 'em. Could have been Max and his Music Hall, I reckon. They've been niggling at us a while.'

'I wish I'd been there,' Angus said. 'It'd make a good story.'

'What, for a stage play?'

'No, no, of course not. Forget what I said.'

There were two more weeks of engagements before the next break and as ill luck would have it their first week coincided with the opening night of Julie's production.

'Well, we can't go.'

Bernard put his foot down.

'It'll have to be the following week.'

'Bernard, we have to,' Eva spoke angrily.

Beth was startled by Eva's vehemence, it was so unlike her. Constance put out her hand.

'Don't worry, we'll read about it in

the papers, then go as soon as we're finished.'

Angus saw how tightly she held Eva's hand. He looked at Beth and saw that she was staring, too. Aunt Eva passed her hand over her eyes.

'Of course, of course, what was I thinking about? We mustn't let our audiences down, especially as things are going quite well again.'

Their next week was Dover. Good audiences, no troubles and Julia's play was opening to good reviews. There was even a mention in the Dover Gazette of Julia Telford in her rôle as Maisie Chivers, a singing, dancing sensation whose family group could be seen nightly at the Assembly Rooms in the town, well worth a visit.

'Who put that in?' Bernard asked in astonishment.

'We did,' Will said. 'Henry's quite a star with the editor's daughter.'

It was in Margate the Telford Tourers received their final blow, and coincidentally it was the same day Angus received a personal telegram from the North of England. He hardly dared believe this was a breakthrough in the search for the lost Lancaster cousin he had been secretly trying to find.

The first couple of days in Margate were quiet enough, then gradually it seemed the rowdy element was at work again. Booing, heckling and slow-handclapping ruined the second half of the show. Bernard seethed and fretted as Constance was greeted by jeers and yells. Families began to leave the hall. One or two tried to quieten the rowdies.

'This is ridiculous,' Angus suddenly said and leaped from stage to floor.

On cue the twins followed.

'Goodness, this is awful,' Constance said and wrung her hands as the fighting spread, but soon the hecklers were in full flight and a cheer went up which quickly hushed as Bernard staggered on to the stage, his face cut and bleeding, his clothes torn.

He tried to speak, his breath

shortened to gasps as he pointed to the dressing-rooms.

'Stolen . . . all gone . . . everything we own . . . police . . .'

Before horrified eyes he collapsed to his knees, rolled slowly over and fell back, grey-faced, barely breathing, a man at the end of his tether.

# 8

Matron herself greeted them at the door of the nursing home. During Bernard's illness she and Constance had become great friends. Constance's charm and concern for her husband quite touched Miss Markham's heart.

'Goodness me, all the family today.'

Her eyebrows rose as Constance, Beth, Clarrie and Aunt Eva crowded into the reception lounge.

'You did say he should be up to more visitors today. That's why they came from Dover.'

Constance took Matron's hand and pressed it affectionately.

'Well, Mr Telford is much improved today,' Matron said. 'Doctor's been and is pleased with him but he did stress there should be no excitement. You can't be too careful after a heart attack like Mr Telford had.'

'We'll be quiet as mice,' Clarrie said, turning her bright eyes on Matron, 'and I haven't seen Daddy since he went poorly on the stage. Please, Matron, I just want to see if he's really here, and well.'

Miss Markham softened.

'Of course he's here. You shall see for yourself my pet, only you mustn't stay long.'

'We won't. As soon as you give the word we'll be off.'

'I'm sure it will do Mr Telford a world of good to see his family.'

'Oh, there are more of us,' Clarrie said, 'only the twins are busy temporarily and of course my sister, Julia, well, she's in the West End.'

'I know. I've seen the show and your sister is wonderful. Such vitality.'

'When can we see London Violets?' Clarrie said.

'We're waiting for your dad to get better,' Eva said. 'Won't it be lovely to go all together? And we have to clear a few things back in Dover first. Don't worry, it won't be long.'

Clarrie looked unconvinced but as soon as Matron ushered them into Bernard's room she forgot everything but the relief of seeing her beloved father sitting up in bed very much alive and smiling broadly at the invasion.

'Well,' Bernard said, 'it is truly wonderful to see you all.'

'You're on the mend,' Constance interrupted. 'Thank goodness Angus called his own doctor and then arranged this nursing home.'

'Do you know, I may not want to come out of here,' Bernard said.

Then his expression changed.

'What's the news in Dover? Have the police found anything? Such a terrible thing to take all our instruments, costumes, props, the lot.'

'Don't worry, Dad, they're only things,' Beth said. 'The worse thing was them hitting you. We can't ever replace you.'

'The fight was deliberately staged to distract us so they, whoever they were, could have taken your equipment,' Constance told him.

'I disturbed them when they were making off with everything. I never saw them, just felt the blow to my head, then I woke up here. Why should anyone go to these extraordinary lengths to close us down?'

There was silence, each individual busy with his or her thoughts then, after a few moments, Bernard announced sadly, 'It's the end then. Telford Tourers is finished. I'm sorry, Constance, if you really want to finish the twelve months I promised then we could perhaps pull ourselves together and carry on.'

'Bernard Telford,' Constance said sharply, 'how dare you! You promised me twelve months but if you even think of keeping that silly promise I'll never speak to you again. How do you think I felt when you collapsed on stage? I thought you'd died and it was my fault. I knew then what was the most important thing in my life. How could I go on living without you?'

She bent her head, choking back tears.

'My dear Constance,' he said, his voice trembling. 'I don't know what to say. You mustn't be upset.'

'I'm not. I'm just happy. These are tears of joy.'

Fortunately, tea arrived at this point and the visit took a much more practical turn as Aunt Eva took over and ticked off her check list.

'I'm so glad you decided but I had to anticipate your decision, Bernard, because the doctor said any more of Telford Tourers could easily kill you. I've cancelled all bookings, sold the carriage, shipped the horses back to pasture at Pikesfell, salvaged a few bits and pieces, and booked us in a London guest house for a few days next week. Julia's booked our seats for London Violets, that is if you're up to it, dear brother. Simple. All done.'

'It sounds like I'm written off as family leader.' Bernard smiled. 'What about the twins, and Jim?'

'Jim's gone to help Nat out at Loughrigg Farm,' Beth put in, 'and Will and Henry are job hunting in London. Angus is helping them.'

No need to bother Dad with her own personal crisis — Nat's letter with a final plea to marry him and go to live at Loughrigg. He missed her so much and she had no excuse now he'd written. Jim's father had told him all about the sabotage and it was inevitable the Telford Tourers should come to an end. The letter had ended simply.

*Our future is here, Beth. All you have to do is to come home and pick it up. I'm afraid I'll always love you. Nat.*

It tore at her heartstrings but she was wracked with indecision and could only reply she had to stay with her family until the Tourers were well and truly finished. She hoped he'd understand.

★   ★   ★

Angus checked his watch a dozen times. The woman he'd contacted had said three o'clock at Euston Station. She was travelling down from the North of England, had business in London and information he could be interested in, but he wasn't to get his hopes up. Her information may have no relevance to his advertisement in The Players' Broadsheet.

The train steamed into the station. She was to be wearing a bright red hat and cloak, the woman had written, to identify herself, but there was no sign of a bright red costume anywhere. Perhaps she had missed the train, perhaps changed her mind or perhaps even it was some cruel hoax. Then he saw her, a middle-aged woman, dark, foreign-looking, strikingly dressed, red cloak, red hat with a long feather, a deferential porter helping her from a first-class carriage, piling luggage on to a trolley.

The woman came straight to Angus, looking him over intently.

'A resemblance,' she said, putting out her hand, 'definitely a resemblance though it's clearly not possible, given the facts of the case. Mrs Rosie Lonsdale at your service. Pleased to meet you, Mr Lancaster. I only have a short time. I've an appointment with my bank manager.'

'The Station Hotel has a fine tea-room,' Angus suggested.

'That's good.'

She pressed silver into the porter's hand.

'Keep an eye on my luggage for a while, would you?'

'Pleasure, ma'am.'

He gasped at the size of the tip as Angus and the woman walked towards the Station Hotel. A few minutes later a man sauntered up to the porter.

'Booked, are you? Woman in the red and the young man? Worth your while just to tip me the wink when she comes back for her luggage.'

The startled porter found yet another tip, this time a ten-shilling note, pressed into his palm. He frowned.

'Not a copper, are you?'

'No. Just need to ask the lady

something. I'll wait in the buffet.'

'All right then. Can't see no wrong in that.'

'Good fellow.'

★   ★   ★

The moment had finally arrived. The entire Telford family and Angus were seated in the best stall seats for the evening performance of London Violets. Beth was suffering terrible stage fright on her sister's behalf and could hardly help herself clutching at Angus who was sitting beside her. He put his hand over hers.

'Stop fidgeting, Beth. Relax and enjoy it.'

But Angus himself was far from calm. Over and over he recalled the woman in red, as vivid now as when he'd spoken to her a week ago, a week of checking the astounding news, letters, telegrams, and still he wasn't sure, couldn't believe what she'd told him.

The curtain swung back for the

opening song of the show. The collective Telfords held their breath as Julia made her entrance.

Angus had booked a private room in a hotel for an after-show supper. They were all very careful of Bernard's health although, watching him now, cheering and clapping, eyes glued to pretty, sparkling Julia bowing and smiling at the curtain call line-up, no-one would believe he'd recently suffered a heart attack.

Aunt Eva and Constance were crying, Clarrie and Beth were open-mouthed at their brilliant sister, and the twins were standing up, stamping and clapping along with the rest of the audience. Beth turned to Angus.

'Isn't she amazing? I can't believe she's my sister. Oh, Angus!'

He put his arm around her, felt her lean into him, then pull away.

'Right,' he said briskly, 'Fred will bring the car round after we've collected Julia from backstage. Julia,' he repeated her name softly, like a puzzled question.

Startled, Beth looked up at him and knew what she'd suspected all along. Angus was in love with her sister and suddenly she had little enthusiasm for the coming celebration. But it was impossible not to join in the wonderful family party which started backstage, with Constance in her element. Tom Brinton, to Constance's joy, actually remembered seeing her on the London stage when he was a young boy.

'No wonder Julia can sing and dance like an angel,' he flattered. 'I never connected her with you. We shall see more of your family then in London?'

'Oh, yes, of course. And Angus is our great friend now. We won't let him go in a hurry.'

'He's very taken with your daughter, isn't he?'

Constance glanced across the crowded dressing-room. Angus was listening to Julia, his eyes never leaving her face.

'Yes, they make a charming pair. Now we really must be leaving. Angus is entertaining us to supper but my husband hasn't been well. There's been so much excitement lately.'

At the end of their delicious supper Bernard stood up to propose a toast.

'First, thanks to Angus for all he's done for this family, second to Julia, our star, in my completely unbiased opinion, of course, and finally to the demise of the Telford Tourers. Happy times and happy memories but now it's time to lay it to rest. New beginnings, a new start for the young ones.'

He raised his glass to the twins.

'And we both have jobs,' Will yelled.

'And Clara's got a lovely sister,' Henry shouted, referring to Will's girlfriend, soon-to-be fiancée.

It was some time before quiet was restored. Bernard held Constance's hand and thought of peaceful Pikesfell. Clarrie was ecstatic at the thought of home and excited at the prospect of a possible double wedding for the twins. Only Eva and Beth looked downcast and Angus, for once, seemed distracted and confused. He couldn't take his eyes off Julia, and Eva, too.

Bernard squeezed his wife's hand. How lucky they were and what a wonderful time it had been, and how marvellous it was to be going home soon. He knew he had to be careful but he and Alf together, with Constance's support, would make a real go of it.

At that moment, Angus stood up and a hush came over the table.

'My days with the Tourers are over. It's been a great experience and I hope we shall remain friends. Before you go, I'd like you to meet my grandfather, Phineas Lancaster. There's something which concerns you, but he's been ill. He's old and frail. I know Bernard wants to get back to Yorkshire as soon as possible but if you can spare another couple of days, relax, see the sights, shopping . . . er . . . Sunday evening perhaps, when there's no show, I'll send the car for you. Martha, my grandfather's housekeeper, will prepare a light supper.'

He stared again at Julia then gave

himself a shake.

'I have to leave now, to call on Grandfather. Fred will take you back to your guest house, whenever you're ready.'

He made as if to leave then stopped behind Constance's chair. She was sitting next to Eva and he addressed them both.

'Especially thank you, Constance and Eva. Thank you.'

And he was gone, leaving the family much puzzled by his exit.

'What did he mean?' Constance asked. 'Why thank Eva and me in particular? We're the ones who should thank him for all he's done for us.'

Eva looked stunned, all colour gone from her face.

'I think perhaps . . . ' she began haltingly.

'Oh, never mind,' Will interrupted picking up a bottle of wine. 'Let's finish this off and Henry and I'll tell you more about our new jobs. Life in London is going to be spiffing.'

# 9

It was almost midnight when Angus arrived at his grandfather's house having telephoned previously to make sure it wasn't too late to look in.

'Phineas'd be very pleased,' Martha had told him, 'but Mr Eric's here again. Your grandfather has been much better this last day or two so I hope your cousin doesn't upset him. He seems reasonable enough just now but you never know with Mr Eric.'

'I'm on my way,' Angus said.

Martha opened the door before he could use his key.

'Thank goodness. I've been watching out for you. They're upstairs.'

'Thanks, Martha. You go on up to bed. I'll probably stay the night.'

'I always keep your old room well aired.' She hesitated. 'Any news?'

'Well, yes, there is, but I've got to

prepare the ground first. I need to tread carefully. It'll be a shock but you'll know soon enough. Oh, we have some visitors on Sunday evening. Could you do a bit of a cold buffet?'

Martha bridled.

'I could do a four-course dinner,' she replied.

Angus couldn't help laughing.

'No aspersions on your cooking, I'd vouch for you, but that wouldn't be appropriate on this occasion. Maybe another time. Good-night, Martha, and don't worry. I'll lock up after Mr Eric's gone.'

'Good-night, Mr Angus.'

'Grandfather,' Angus greeted the old man who was propped high on pillows, and nodded to his cousin. 'Eric, a bit late for a visit.'

'But all right for you, I suppose. Nothing you do is ever wrong, of course.'

Angus sighed.

'I didn't come here to quarrel with you.'

'Why have you come then? To check on me?'

'Goodness' sake, don't be so edgy. I came to see how Grandfather is.'

'Better, better,' the old gentleman replied. 'Much improved as you can see. Eric here is still worried about his inheritance. Doesn't fancy a three-way split, but I hope that's what it will be. Found him yet?' he asked eagerly.

'Not exactly.'

Angus didn't want to tell Phineas the news yet, not with Eric present.

'It's very late, Grandfather. You should get some sleep. I'll talk to you in the morning. I'm staying here for a couple of days, just to keep an eye on you before I go on my travels again.'

'Ah, you leaving the country then?'

Eric had a very strange look about him which Angus didn't like. He knew Eric of old. It was his cat's-got-the-cream look and it usually meant trouble.

'I think it best if we let Grandfather sleep now,' he said pointedly.

'I'm sure you do. You always did know best. All right, I'm off.'

He turned to Phineas.

'And that's final, is it? If this boy is ever found, he's to have equal shares in the Lancaster fortune?'

'Eric, I've told you several times over. My mind's made up and I'll not shift. The boy is a Lancaster and as such will share the inheritance. Good heavens, man, there's plenty there. Our chief accountant is due to visit for the annual audit. You should know more than anyone the state of our financial health. Now run along and stop fretting.'

Eric's lips were pressed tightly together, his eyes glittered with anger.

'I won't be treated like this. I'll show both of you I mean business.'

Eric always did insist on the final word. He slammed the door.

'I'm sorry, Grandfather.'

'Oh, I don't mind him, not any more. I'm too old to worry about Eric's tantrums. Now, won't you tell me the developments in the search? My grand-son . . . '

But two seconds later he was snoring, evenly and gently as a baby. Angus tip-toed from the room. He had very little sleep that night. He went through his files time and time again, checking for any possible flaws in the story of Rosie Lonsdale, the lady in red, but he could find none.

Dawn was edging the sky with light before he finally settled to sleep, knowing that incredible as it seemed, the search for Albert Lancaster was over. He only hoped his grandfather would be happy with what he'd found.

At the Telfords' guest house, Bernard and Constance proposed a day of gentle sightseeing.

'Nothing too strenuous,' Constance decreed. 'Dear Angus has put Fred and his motor at our disposal so it shouldn't be too exhausting.'

Eva had opted to stay and work on the final accounts of the Tourers.

'Don't forget, I lived and worked in

London for years before I came to Pikesfell. I've seen most of its sights several times over.'

Beth chose to stay with Aunt Eva. She needed a confidante more than a sightseeing trip.

Eva Telford worked for an hour but found it hard to concentrate. There was something on her mind she couldn't quite put her finger on, besides which she sensed Beth herself was unsettled. She put down her pen and closed the ledger.

'Beth, why are we mouldering indoors on such a lovely summer day? We should have a holiday, too. Let's take a tram to the park, buy some buns and have a picnic.'

'Nothing I'd like better.'

They sat in the bright sunshine, ate their buns and fed the ducks the remains. Eva screwed up her eyes against the sun.

'Have you decided what you are going to choose, Beth, town or country? I know Nat's written to you again so that door's not closed.'

'I feel bad about Nat. I just can't decide.'

'If you can't decide, he's not right for you. Marriage is a lifetime commitment. On the other hand . . . '

'What?'

Beth put her elbows on her knees, and listened carefully to her pet aunt.

'Is anything perfect? Sometimes I think we have to compromise. Nat loves you. You love the country, farming would suit you, and lots of children. Doesn't sound too bad.'

'Surely there are other things first. You had a good career, didn't you?'

'Yes, I did. I travelled all over, loved it, but look at me now. No family of my own, only lots of picture postcards of places I've already forgotten. Nothing permanent.'

'You've us, Aunt Eva. Aren't we enough?'

'I'm very lucky to have you all, but sometimes we're given an important choice in life and sometimes we make the wrong choice. We have to learn to live with it. You're at that point, Beth. Nat's given you a second chance. Think hard about it before you make your choice.'

'I've thought and thought until my head aches and I don't think what I feel for Nat is truly love. Did you make the right choices in your life?'

'Probably not on the whole, but life has a habit of working out all right. Old age has its compensations, wisdom, acceptance of what life brings.'

'I don't think I'm ready for acceptance yet and I've never had to make an important decision in my life so far.'

'Well, now's the time. You have to make some positive decisions. It's not fair to keep poor Nat dangling. You've made some good decisions lately. Your new hairstyle is lovely, that dress suits you beautifully. There's a new Beth emerging. All you have to do is decide what you want to do with her.'

'I'll try. I quite envy Julia. Her decisions have been made for her.'

'I shouldn't envy her. A life in showbusiness can be desperately hard.'

'But she has Angus, too.'

'Angus? What's he to do with it?'

'They're in love. Surely everyone can see that. Isn't that what meeting Angus's grandfather is all about?'

'Is it? There is something in the wind but . . . maybe you're right. Let's wait and see, shall we? Right now, why don't we simply enjoy this lovely sunshine and take a walk around the lake? Just remember though, be honest with yourself, look in your heart and ask just why you can't accept Nat and settle down to family life.'

Beth looked away. Her aunt's last words had struck home. She daren't be honest with herself because deep down she knew the reason she could never love Nat. She wouldn't admit it, but she realised she must do the right thing and tell Nat she couldn't marry him. She didn't love him and never could. The reason, she locked firmly away in her heart.

★   ★   ★

Bernard had decided to leave for Pikes-fell the day after the visit to Angus's grandfather. There was no further business concerning the Tourers. The police had made no headway on the burglary and assault. There was little point in staying in London.

The twins were to start their new jobs the following week and had already settled in lodgings. The family was splitting up, sad but inevitable, and Bernard was anxious to make his own fresh start at Pikesfell. Constance decided on a last shopping expedition.

'Beth and I need new clothes suitable for the country and Julia's wardrobe needs a complete make-over. Don't worry, Bernard, we'll bargain-hunt like mad.'

Beth was hesitant. Buying country clothes, whatever Constance meant by that, symbolised a decision she hadn't finalised. She'd already written to Nat, but whether she was really ready for a spinster life in the Yorkshire Fells or not was a different matter. Maybe she'd stay a while, follow the twins' example, look for a job. Sample city life!

'Do come with us, Beth, dear,' Constance pleaded. 'We'll have the whole morning before Julia's matinée performance. Perhaps we could see London Violets again in the afternoon, then lunch in town. Bernard and Eva are taking Clarrie to the zoo.'

'Yes, I'd like to see the show again.'

The three women set out for Oxford Street in high spirits.

'London is such fun.'

Julia practically danced along the pavements.

'I love living here, though I'll miss you all dreadfully,' she added quickly, seeing her mother's face. 'Beth, why don't you stay for a while? There are lots of jobs you could do and we could find lodgings together.'

'Maybe one day,' Beth hedged, thinking Julia wouldn't stay a free agent long enough for that.

Angus would surely declare his love very soon. The thought was painful.

Constance swept them through the doors of a large department store.

'Third floor, coats and dresses. I know just what I want.'

As it happened, it took longer than she'd bargained for. Beth and Julia became bored.

'Ma, we'll nip downstairs to the ground floor. There's some lovely costume jewellery and I do need a new necklace. Come on, Beth, we'll meet up in half an hour in the tea-room.'

Constance turned this way and that in front of the dressing-room mirror.

'All right. Don't get lost.'

The two girls were soon lost amongst the jewellery counters.

'Let's buy something for Clarrie.'

Beth picked up a bracelet.

'She'd love this. It's amber, isn't it?'

'Just right for Clarrie. I can't find the right necklace. I've seen it somewhere. I know, in the window, on that model. I'll go and look while you

152

buy the bracelet for Clarrie.'

'No, wait. I'll come with you.'

Too late, Julia had disappeared among the crowd of shoppers.

'Did you want to buy that?'

An assistant looked suspiciously at Beth, still holding the amber bracelet.

'Yes, yes, I do, but my sister's got my purse. She's just gone to look at the window display.'

'Well, I'll just take it back for now. Perhaps when your sister returns . . . '

The assistant's expression indicated she didn't believe a word of it and if Beth didn't clear off, she'd call the manager. Colour rose in Beth's cheeks. She swallowed back an angry retort and looked around for Julia. The window display was close by. She should be back by now.

With a terrible sense of unease, Beth turned and ran out of the store, jostling customers aside, pushing back rising anxiety. Julia was quite capable of looking after herself but why wasn't she outside? There was no-one by the

153

jewellery window. She saw the necklace Julia wanted. Perhaps she was back inside the shop. Beth went back to the counter.

'Have you seen my sister?' she queried the assistant.

'You again,' the woman said coldly. 'I don't know your sister, but no-one's been here since you left.'

Beth dashed outside again, looking up and down the street. There was no sign of Julia. She must have gone inside and they'd missed each other. That was it, she'd be in the tea-room waiting for her. As she stood irresolutely on the pavement, a man with a violin came up to her. She'd noticed him as they were going into the store. Constance had dropped some coins in his box.

'You looking for someone?' he said. 'Young girl, blonde, very pretty? Came in with you and the older lady earlier?'

'Yes, yes, my sister. I've lost her.'

'She went off in a car. Looking in that window she was, and a man came up to her, talked for a bit, took her arm and put her in the car. Drove off like the wind. I didn't like it at the time but she didn't shout or scream so I kept out of it. Best get your mother, or call the police, I would. I'll be off. Hope you find your sister. Such a pretty girl.'

'Wait, no, you can't go. The man, who was he? What did he look like? Oh, please, come back.'

She ran after him but he disappeared among the crowds.

# 10

Constance waved when she saw Beth running towards her, calling out, 'I'm sorry I've been so long. Miss Pelham here's been marvellous, fitted me with a completely new . . . why what's wrong, Beth. Where's Julia?'

'She's gone. Someone's taken her in a car.'

'Gone? In a car? You're not making sense. Calm down and tell me what's happened.'

Beth told her everything. Constance closed her eyes, sent a brief prayer heavenwards, then snapped into action.

'Miss Pelham, call your manager, please, and the store detective. It could simply be that Julia was distracted and is in another part of the store. That fiddler outside may have mischievously invented the man in the car. I cannot imagine Julia leaving against her will in a stranger's vehicle. The store should be searched first, and the tea-room, obviously.'

The store's personnel couldn't have been more helpful or concerned especially when Constance told them the missing girl was due on stage in just three hours. But there was no trace of Julia in the store.

'The police, madam?' the manager enquired.

Constance hesitated.

'I think it best if we go back to our lodgings. My husband will know what to do, but thank all your staff for their help.'

It was only when the cab was nearly at the guesthouse that they remembered Bernard and Eva had taken Clarrie to the zoo and wouldn't be back until tea time. For the first time, Constance's composure crumbled.

'Beth, what shall we do?'

'Call the police at once, and look, thank goodness, there's Angus's car outside the house.'

He came out to meet them.

'I called to confirm tomorrow. Constance, what's wrong? Beth, what's happened?'

'It's Julia! She's disappeared. We can't find her. We went shopping . . . '

Angus looked relieved.

'But she's probably at the theatre. Isn't there a matinée Saturday?'

'No,' Constance almost screamed. 'Someone took her in a car and she's not at the theatre. The manager of the store checked. You tell him, Beth, I just can't think straight any more.'

Angus took Constance indoors, ordered hot tea with a shot of brandy and went straight to the telephone. Beth was pouring tea when he came back and sat on the sofa next to Constance.

'You stay here, wait for Bernard and Eva, but don't alarm them. Tell the police exactly what Beth told me. I've been in touch with the theatre and the London Evening News and they're going to run Julia's description, also the man with the violin's story. The street was busy, Beth said, so somebody must have seen something. Beth, you must come with me. We'll look for the violinist. I know that area well, and just about every busker in the place. If he was lying, I'll soon know. Will you come?'

'Of course. Mother, will you be all right? Dad and Aunt Eva shouldn't be too long. I'm sure this is all a ghastly mistake. Julia will turn up, I know it.'

'I wish I could be as certain. But go, go quickly.'

'How do you think you can find the man?' Beth asked in the car. 'There are dozens of streets and back alleys.'

'I know exactly where to look. We'll start here and if you spot him tell me at once.'

The pub they went to in a dingy back street was crowded with regulars who all stared at Angus and Beth when they walked in.

'Have a look round,' Angus told her. 'I'll talk to the landlord.'

'Mr Lancaster,' the publican beamed.

'What can I do for you?'

They conferred briefly, the landlord nodded, pointed up the street and shook Angus by the hand.

'Best of luck,' he called after them.

Three more pubs they visited, one hostel, then the Salvation Army shelter, but no luck. Angus looked at his watch.

'Damn, what a fool! It's obvious. The first place I should have looked.'

He drove back to Oxford Street, and there was the violinist scraping away a discreet distance from the main entrance to the department store.

'He's doing the afternoon shift,' Angus murmured. 'Don't alarm him or he'll make a run for it.'

Beth hung back as Angus went up to the man and dropped a coin in his violin case. Startled by its value the man stopped playing, looked up, saw Beth and bent to pick up his earnings.

'Must run,' he muttered.

'No, you don't.'

Angus put his foot over the case.

'Just a word, and I'm not a

policeman. There's more money for you if you can describe the man who took this young lady's sister this morning.'

'She not found yet? Oh, dear. I hope no harm's come to her. But she didn't struggle, just pulled a face, like it was all a nuisance.'

'The man, can you describe him?'

'Certainly can, and his mate, the driver. Had the engine running, finger tapping on the wheel, in a hurry to be off. Man who spoke to the young lady was about six foot . . . '

Halfway through the musician's detailed description of the driver Angus stopped him.

'That's it. I know who it is. You've been a great help.'

He pressed a note into the man's hand.

'Thanks. I hope she's all right, the young lady.'

'She'd better be, but thanks to you I know what I'm up against.'

'What did he tell you,' Beth asked anxiously, 'about the man who took her? Shouldn't you tell the police?'

'Probably, but the repercussions would be undesirable.'

'But Julia, she could be anywhere. Anything could have happened.'

He opened the car door for her.

'Beth, you'll just have to trust me. I can't explain yet but I can assure you I don't think Julia's in any real danger. I should be able to find her before the day's out. Do you want me to take you back to your mother?'

'I'd rather come with you if it'll lead to Julia. Better than sitting around waiting for news.'

'All right. Just one thing, no questions. If I'm right and we find Julia tonight I'll explain everything, and I mean everything. Agreed?'

'I don't think I have a choice.'

'You're right.'

As they drove through the streets Beth didn't even feel like asking questions. She trusted Angus to find her sister and that was all that mattered. He stopped eventually outside an elegant block of flats, got out of the car and asked her to wait.

'Julia's here?' she asked incredulously.

'No, only the remotest chance, but I want to check something.'

He was gone a quarter of an hour and when he came back out of the building Beth was waiting on the pavement looking up at the building and wondering if by any chance Julia was behind one of those closely-curtained windows, held against her will. Angus put his arms round her.

'Sorry, it took a little longer than I expected. Don't be frightened.'

'Not in there?' she stated.

'No, I didn't expect it.'

'So now where?'

'You'll see. No questions, remember.'

He drove south towards the river and in other circumstances Beth would have loved watching the people on the streets, strolling in the golden evening sunshine, enjoying their Saturday evening leisure. Her own morning shopping expedition seemed centuries away.

'Where are we? It's pretty.'

'Richmond. Did you never come this way with the Tourers?'

'No. Mainly the resorts along the coast. It was Mother's ambition, London. The nearer to London, the happier she was. Angus, why are we here chatting politely while anything could be happening to Julia?'

He stopped the car, got out and opened the door.

'Because if we don't, I may do something rash, and then regret it. I need you to be calm and again I say you have to trust me. We'll walk along the towpath now by the river, about two miles.'

The coiled spring of his anger was tautly stretched, his hands clenched by his side, only unclenched to stop her from stumbling as the path got rougher. They'd been walking about an hour when the path stopped abruptly and the river widened behind a **Private Land, No Trespassing** sign. A rough landing stage jutted out from a wooden boathouse.

Beth looked around. It was almost dusk but she could make out a cottage in the distance and a path running from boathouse to cottage.

'Here?' Beth asked, amazed.

'Most likely up at the cottage, Eric's country retreat. It's 'way off the beaten track.'

'I don't understand.'

'Listen.'

Angus held up his hand. A voice yelled out from the boathouse.

'Anyone there? Help, help, inside here. Ahoy!'

'It's Julia! Oh, we're coming. It's Beth and Angus.'

But Angus was already there, hammering on the door.

'Julia, can you let us in? The door, it's locked.'

'I can't, I'm tied up. The key's on the inside.'

'Are you alone?'

'Yes.'

He put his shoulder to the door and lunged. The wood splintered. Beth picked up a boat hook from a tethered punt and thrust it through the splintered wood, then Angus put his hand into the hole and turned the key. The room was dim. Julia was sitting on a bed, wrists and ankles bound. He took her in his arms, hugging her closely to him.

'Are you all right? Not hurt? Where is he? If he's harmed you I'll kill him.'

'Eric? He said he was your cousin. What on earth's this all about? Beth!'

They embraced, Beth and Angus far more agitated than Julia.

'He made me promise to wait and then he was going to send someone to let me out, but he had to get away. Angus, is he truly your cousin, and is he a little bit mad?'

'Both, dear Julia.'

He stroked her hair tenderly.

'I'm so sorry he put you through this.'

'I wasn't scared. He was quite nice

until he started ranting on about getting his own back, always being blamed. I didn't like the other fellow, the one who told me I was urgently wanted at the theatre and he'd get a message to you, Beth. But we dropped him off in London and Eric drove me here. See, he's left me lots of food, even some wine. I wasn't frightened. He was kind of sad, Eric, I mean.'

'Thank God you're all right.'

Angus kept tight hold of her.

'You'll be home before you know it. Julia, if only you knew . . . '

He pressed her to him and kissed her on the forehead.

'If only you knew what a precious commodity you are.'

'The worst thing is, I've missed the show, two whole performances. What'll Tom Brinton say? I still don't know why . . . '

Angus was cutting through the ropes.

'Tom will understand and I expect your understudy will have been delighted. I promise I'll explain everything tomorrow at my grandfather's house, but we'll get you home now. Can you manage to walk?'

'Goodness, yes, I've had a good long rest here, quite an adventure really. Are you really sure Eric's your cousin? You're not a bit alike.'

'Thank goodness for that.'

Julia eventually was snuggled down in the back of the car covered in a rug and in spite of her protestations that she wasn't the least tired she fell fast asleep just outside Richmond.

So many questions buzzed in Beth's head but one look at Angus's dark profile and she knew she wouldn't get any answers that night. He kept glancing in the back of the car as if to make sure Julia was really safe. He'd stopped at the nearest police station to report Julia's safety and asked them to let Bernard and Constance know. He didn't speak until they were almost at the guesthouse.

Then he said quietly, 'I hope you'll be happy with Nat, Beth. Constance told me you'd made it up and you'd be going back to Yorkshire.'

'Mother told you that?'

'Yes, she thinks it'll be right for you. He does love you, doesn't he?'

'He tells me so.'

They were almost at the guest house and all the lights were on.

'And you love Julia, Angus. I hope you'll be happy, too.'

Tears threatened and she swallowed hard.

'There's no-one I'd like better as a brother-in-law.'

He stopped the car and lifted his hands from the wheel.

'Brother-in-law? Julia? What are you talking about?'

'Why, you and Julia. Anyone can see you're in love.'

'Beth Telford, I took you for an intelligent and perceptive woman. Julia! I do love her, in a brotherly way. She's pretty and bright and of course I love her, but not romantically. In any case, if I did it wouldn't be appropriate.'

He took Beth's face in his hands.

'I couldn't marry her even if I wanted to. Julia Telford is my cousin.'

Just then Julia woke up.

'Are we home already? Look, they're all there on the front steps. Goodness, I feel like royalty. What's the matter, Beth? You're looking odd.'

Then she was enveloped by her family who practically dragged her into the house. Bernard helped Beth out.

'Angus,' he said, 'we can't thank you enough, again. We'd like you to come in and tell us what happened but there's an urgent message from a Mrs Clarke. You're to go home at once. She says to tell you your grandfather isn't ill but he's had a letter, special delivery from a Mr Eric.'

'I'll go at once. We'll see you tomorrow unless you hear from me. Goodnight, Bernard, Beth.'

The car roared up the street leaving Beth standing on the pavement in total bewilderment.

'Mr Eric?' she repeated. 'That's his cousin, too. How could Julia possibly be

Angus's cousin? And if she's Angus's cousin she's also Eric's cousin. No, this is a nightmare and I'll wake up in a minute and we'll be about to go on stage at Grimston, except that'd be an even worse nightmare. Oh, Dad, I don't understand one bit.'

'Never mind, we're all here together, safe and sound. Come and have some supper. It's been a long day.'

Next morning Angus telephoned the guesthouse and spoke to Bernard.

'No ill effects, I hope?'

'No. Julia's in fine spirits, Beth rather subdued, Constance still having palpitations. It'll be some time before she goes shopping again.'

'I'm so sorry to have put you through this ordeal.'

'It wasn't your fault, Angus.'

'It was, and I must explain things to you. I've already spoken to my grandfather. He declares he can't wait until this evening to meet you all. Could you come sooner? I'll send the car.'

'Soon as you like. We've talked

ourselves dry speculating on your cousin's motives.'

'Half an hour then. Has Beth said anything?'

'No. Should she have done?'

'Fine. Half an hour.'

Beth hadn't mentioned Angus's comment about Julia and him being cousins because she truly believed she must have misheard it. It was ludicrous, quite impossible.

Fred drew up exactly thirty minutes later but even the Lancasters' spacious limousine couldn't accommodate all the Telfords so Aunt Eva and the twins followed in a hired cab to Phineas's imposing house overlooking Hampstead Heath. The family was overawed by it.

'Rather big for one person,' Julia said.

Angus met them at the door and introduced them to Martha Clarke.

'Martha's been with us since she was a young girl. She had a part to play in the story I have to tell. My grandfather is still in some shock but it's a happy shock. He's in the drawing-room.'

He led them to a large, sunny room overlooking spacious lawns and fine flower beds. Phineas was seated in an upright chair by the fireplace. He rose when the Telfords entered, leaning heavily on his stick, searching their faces.

'Grandfather, this is the Telford family. I've told you all about them.'

Phineas nodded.

'You're all very welcome.'

His voice was strained, rusty-sounding. He looked up at Angus.

'Where is . . . '

Angus took Julia's hand and led her forward.

'Julia, this will come as a shock to you. This gentleman is your grandfather, Phineas Lancaster.'

The old man gasped and put out a hand to Angus.

'But it's Mary, our daughter, Mary.'

All colour gone, he collapsed back into the chair and covered his face. The younger Telfords looked puzzled, but

Constance, Bernard and Eva knew that, bizarre as it sounded, it could be possible.

'What does he mean?' Julia asked, turning to her parents. 'My grandparents are dead.'

The twins stared at Angus.

Henry said, 'Julia's our sister. That man can't be our grandfather.'

'Martha,' Angus said to her, 'drinks?'

'All ready.'

She pulled a bell cord.

A hubbub rose. Julia clung to her mother, Eva looked despairing. The arrival of a drinks trolley brought a useful pause and after a glass of sherry Julia began to glance curiously at Phineas.

Constance said, 'I think we're ready now to hear your explanation, Angus.'

He nodded.

'To begin with, it's not an unusual tale. Twenty-two years ago, my unmarried Aunt Mary left home. She was pregnant.'

'I turned her out. Don't spare me,'

Phineas interrupted.

Angus ignored his grandfather.

'Mary disappeared, no-one knows where but when the child was nearly twelve months old she wrote to her mother who tried to reconcile father and daughter. For a short while Eliza and Mary remained in secret contact, then Mary met up with a band of strolling players and travelled North with them. Her family never heard from her again.'

'How awful,' Constance said, 'but I don't understand what it has to do with us.'

Angus looked at Eva.

'Can't you guess? The child Eva brought to Pikesfell was Mary's, Julia.'

'Aunt Eva brought me to Pikesfell?' Julia cried out.

'I did,' Eva said and took up the story. 'Your mother, Mary Lancaster, had died and for a while the group cared for you, but business was bad, money ran out and they disbanded. The only option for Mary's child, you, was an orphanage, until I met Rosie Lonsdale, who helped me so much. You see, I was at a low ebb after a disastrous love affair. I thought my salvation would be a child, and here was a child looking for a home. I took you gladly.'

Angus said, 'I met Rosie Lonsdale last week. She answered an advertisement I'd placed in the Players' Broadsheet.'

'But you said a boy, Albert Lancaster,' Beth cried.

'Albert was the name Martha had heard my grandmother say when she was dying. We just assumed . . . but Mary had named the baby Albertine, after the popular Prince Albert. So I'd been looking all the while for a young man until I saw Julia on stage and had this terrible sense of déja vu. I knew that face. Of course it was a memory imprint from my boyhood, of Aunt Mary.'

'You took me, Aunt Eva,' Julia said.

'Yes. I wanted so much to keep you but I soon realised it would have been sheer foolishness, a single woman with no money. I needed a job and London was where the jobs were. So I went to Yorkshire and brought you to Bernard and Constance who immediately accepted you as their own child.'

'Beth was a baby so you were a ready-made big sister. When we adopted you we called you Julia. I hope you don't mind,' Constance said.

Julia shook her head.

'I can't take this in. Over twenty years — did no-one in the village know?'

'I believe some of them may have thought you were Eva's, but nobody cared. You were always a Telford.'

There was an uneasy pause.

'And now I'm not,' Julia said in a small voice.

'Of course you are, by upbringing.'

'We never expected to find Albert was a young lady in a warm and loving family,' Angus said. 'Perhaps we should have thought of that possibility before disrupting your lives.'

'I just wanted to make amends, put it right,' Phineas said sadly.

'Perhaps,' Bernard said tactfully, 'we should see it as Julia gaining another family.'

'And Cousin Eric?' Julia asked.

'Eric's caused a lot of trouble,' Angus said. 'He was on to me from the start and didn't want me to find Albert because it jeopardised his inheritance. When I joined the Tourers he was sure I'd got close, and he was responsible for all the sabotage. He even got to Rosie Lonsdale at the station where I met her and made her tell him Mary's story. He had some wild idea of holding Julia hostage until Grandfather promised not to put you in his will.'

'His will! I don't want any money,' Julia said, looking horrified. 'I'm going to be a famous actress. Oh, dear, poor Eric, I do feel quite sorry for him.'

'Don't,' Angus said grimly. 'He has absconded with a large chunk of Grandfather's money and he's been milking the business for years. He was frightened once Phineas started looking into things and realised the game was up. He wrote a confession last night before he left the country. Don't worry about Eric. He usually manages to land on his feet.'

'But he's my family,' Julia said. 'Today I've exchanged a mother, father, aunt, two sisters, two brothers for . . . well, two cousins and a grandad.'

Howls of protest drowned her as she was smothered in hugs and kisses from any Telford who could reach any bit of her. An awful groaning, keening sound cut through the noise as Phineas, head in hands, rocked back.

'Lord, forgive me, I've done wrong again. Mary . . . Julia . . . I never meant to cause distress. Angus, can't we undo all this?'

The old man's face was pitiful. Angus kneeled by his chair.

'No, we can't. Perhaps it was a mistake but we can't go back. It's been a terrible shock for Julia. Give her time.'

But Julia, too, was kneeling, next to Angus.

'Mr Lancaster, Grandad, oh, dear. I didn't mean to upset you.'

She laid her head on his knee and burst into tears. There was silence in the room as Julia's sobs quietened and very gradually, fearfully, Phineas Lancaster put out a hand and rested it on his granddaughter's blonde curls.

'There, there, I'm sorry, too.'

A tentative pat, then a surer touch followed as he bent to lift her head.

'We'll get to know each other. I make no demands, just to see you, to help maybe, you and your family if Eric's left anything in the coffers. Don't be proud. I can do something for your family, your proper family. I've no rights, no rights at all. What Eric said was true. I am a foolish, old man.'

With his hand still on Julia's head he spoke to all her family.

'Please, stay with me today. We can get acquainted. I'm a lonely, old man in this great house.'

Constance got up and went to him.

'Of course we'll stay. We're going back to Yorkshire tomorrow, Bernard, Eva and me, Clarrie, too, but the twins will visit, and Julia, of course, and you'll come to us at Pikesfell, before the summer's out, if possible.'

She leaned down and kissed him.

'Phineas, I bless the day you sent Angus on his mission to find 'Albert'. It's enriched our lives and I'm sure will continue to do so.'

Phineas smiled and a tear lurked in the corner of his eye.

Tentatively he said, 'It's a beautiful day. Perhaps I can show you the garden. There's an ornamental pond, a tennis court, not used, I fear.'

He got to his feet, reached for his stick but Will and Henry beat him to it, offering an arm on each side.

'We're hot on tennis, sir. Perhaps we can have a game some day soon.'

Slowly the Telfords followed but Angus caught Beth's arm.

'I need to ask you something,' he murmured.

'About Julia? She'll be all right. She's always taken life in her stride. She'll manage her two families beautifully, maybe even reform Eric.'

'Now that would be a miracle.'

'Don't you think this whole thing's a miracle, the whole story? Julia, Albert, rather Albertine, that is, it's all incredible.'

Angus took her in his arms.

'I don't want to ask about Julia. I want to ask about you, and what I find incredible is that in searching for Albert Lancaster for Phineas I should find Beth Telford. Before I say anything else, I have to know about Nat. Are you to marry him?'

'No. I wrote last week. Nat's always been a good friend but I couldn't marry him.'

'Why not?' Angus asked, anxious to hear her answer.

'Because I don't love him.'

'How can you tell, about love? You thought I loved Julia.'

'I didn't know she was your cousin then.'

'And now?'

His dark eyes held hers, his arms tightened around her and he kissed her, that sweet sensation again, overpowering, powerful, irresistible, and she knew without doubt it was a kiss of true love.

'Angus . . . what . . . '

'No more questions, Beth. Just answer mine. Nothing else matters. I love you, always did from that moment in Brighton, by the sea. Your face in the moonlight has haunted me ever since. It's you I've thought of constantly, not Julia. I love you. Will you marry me?'

She raised her eyes to his, breathless with happiness.

'Of course I will marry you. I love you, too, and knew I could never marry Nat because it was you I loved, always.'

As the voices of the Telfords and Lancasters mingled in the sunlit garden beyond the drawing-room, Angus kissed Beth passionately, a kiss which held the promise of mutual love for ever.

We do hope that you have enjoyed reading this large print book.

Did you know that all of our titles are available for purchase?

We publish a wide range of high quality large print books including:
**Romances, Mysteries, Classics**
**General Fiction**
**Non Fiction and Westerns**

Special interest titles available in large print are:
**The Little Oxford Dictionary**
**Music Book, Song Book**
**Hymn Book, Service Book**

Also available from us courtesy of Oxford University Press:
**Young Readers' Dictionary**
**(large print edition)**
**Young Readers' Thesaurus**
**(large print edition)**

For further information or a free brochure, please contact us at:
**Ulverscroft Large Print Books Ltd.,**
**The Green, Bradgate Road, Anstey,**
**Leicester, LE7 7FU, England.**
**Tel:** (00 44) **0116 236 4325**
**Fax:** (00 44) **0116 234 0205**

# THE PERFECT GENTLEMAN

## Liz Pedersen

When Laura agrees to help Anthony
Christopher to deceive his family
she has no idea how far the web of
intrigue will extend, or how it will
alter her life. His family is as
unpleasant as he promised, but
Laura drives away from his funeral
thinking she has escaped their
malicious clutches. However, this is
not so. James Christopher is determined to discover what was behind
his cousin's precipitate marriage. He
despises Laura and hates the fact
that he is attracted to her.

# YESTERDAY'S LOVE

## Stella Ross

Jessica's return from Africa to claim her inheritance of 'Simon's Cottage', and take up medicine in her home town, is the signal for her past to catch up with her. She had thought the short affair she'd had with her cousin Kirk twelve years ago a long-forgotten incident. But Kirk's unexpected return to England, on a last-hope mission to save his dying son, sparks off nostalgia. It leads Jessica to rethink her life and where it is leading.